MW01680959

UNEARTHING CROCODOPOLIS

RICK AND ROSE SINCLAIR ADVENTURE #5

RUSSELL JAMES

SEVEREDPRESS

UNEARTHING CROCODOPOLIS

WWW.SEVEREDPRESS.COM

ISBN: 978-1-923663-35-0

Other books by Russell James

Rick and Rose Sinclair Adventures

Quest for the Queen's Temple
Voyage to Blackbeard's Island
Quest for the City of Gold
Passage Up the Mekong

Grant Coleman Adventures

Cavern of the Damned
Monsters in the Clouds
Curse of the Viper King
Forest of Fire
Mammoth Island
Atoll X
Desolation Canyon
River of Death
Terror on Mount St. Helens

Ranger Kathy West National Park Adventures

Claws
Dragons of Kilauea
Ravens of Yellowstone

DEDICATION

For Christy,
My Rose on every adventure

CHAPTER ONE

1302 BC
Thirty miles north of Lake Moeris, Egypt.

The pharaoh sighed. The sentry scrambling down the steep escarpment across from her camp could only be bringing her bad news.

The sun beat down hard and hot onto the awning under which Pharaoh Sobekneferu sat on a golden chair. Slaves beside her waved large fans but that provided little relief from the heat. Her trusted high priestess, Mut-em-menu, stood nearby while a scribe sat at the female pharaoh's feet, awaiting any decrees or conversations that needed to be recorded.

Around her tent, a century of her palace guards checked their weapons and inspected their chariots. Despite ruling all the lands of the kingdom of Egypt, this small force was all she could muster when she received the warnings of the impending coup.

Since her rise to power four years earlier, she had expected a rebellion. Being the first female pharaoh to lead Egypt, she had not been universally accepted by the elites or the military. Sobekneferu didn't need spies or soothsayers to tell her that. She could feel intrigue in the air from her first day on the throne. With no earthly power to support her, she had turned to the gods, or one god in particular. She'd sensed a kindred spirit in Sobek, the crocodile-headed god of the Nile, imprisoned by his fellow gods.

Through her beloved Mut-em-menu, Sobekneferu had contacted the god. He looked upon the pharaoh with favor and his interventions had helped Sobekneferu on many occasions. In return, she had built the massive city of Crocodopolis as both a tribute to him, and as a doorway for his return. Then she would destroy the mortals who opposed her, and Sobek would vanquish the gods who had caged him.

But as she had fled the capitol yesterday, it was clear that her enemies had curried the favor of even more powerful gods.

The sentry stumbled in under Sobekneferu's awning and fell to one knee. "Your Majesty."

"Arise and report," Sobekneferu said.

"A cloud of dust rises in the north. An army approaches."

"Just as I warned you," Mut-em-menu said.

Sobekneferu still held out hope that the bulk of the military had refused to rebel against the royal house. "How many soldiers?"

The sentry took a deep breath and answered through gritted teeth. "It seems like all of them, my Queen."

Sobekneferu closed her eyes and lowered her head. She wondered how things had gotten so out of hand so quickly. She looked back up at the sentry. "Return to your post. Report back when they are two miles away."

The sentry saluted and withdrew.

"We can still win this," Mut-em-menu said. "We have the power of Sobek on our side."

"Not all his power. We have not resurrected him yet. I cannot hold off an entire army with a hundred palace guards."

"But I can," Mut-em-menu said. "You and the guards wait here. No one but the two of us know of this secluded location. I will take a charioteer and have him return me to the pass north of here. I will call on Sobek to crumble the escarpment into the pass and seal it. Then I will return to you. The only other route to Crocodopolis is up the Nile, and it will take them days to backtrack and do that."

Sobekneferu smiled. "And by then we will have called forth Sobek, and he will smite the entire army with one blow."

"And you will rule Egypt forever. I should bring the enchanted amulet with me to give me the best connection to Sobek."

Sobekneferu clutched at the amulet that hung from a chain around her neck. A metal figure eight encased two brilliant, twin sapphires. The chain attached to little loops at each end. The two sapphires pulsed with a blue glow. This amulet was the key that, along with the power of their souls, could open the passage for Sobek's return. She could not entrust it to Mut-em-menu if the priestess was going to confront the rebel army.

But she also could not send her priestess out alone without the amulet's connection to Sobek.

Sobekneferu unfastened the chain and pinched one sapphire with each hand. She flexed the amulet and the figure eight snapped in half. The light in the sapphires dimmed. She handed one half of the amulet to Mut-em-menu.

"Go forth and save your queen," she said.

"I will," Mut-em-menu said, "and then I will return. No matter how long it takes me, we will rejoin these jewels in Crocodopolis and together bring forth Sobek."

CHAPTER TWO

1938
Savannah, Georgia

Rick Sinclair stepped out of the jeweler's shop on Bay Street and grinned. His coat pocket bulged with cash.

He checked his reflection in the glass and carefully donned his fedora without messing the razor-sharp part to his hair. He gave his pencil mustache a stroke with his finger and began the short walk back to the antiques shop he and his wife Rose owned.

The two of them had just returned from a wild adventure tracking down a jade hand that had been stolen from them. It turned out it had been stolen from someone else before Rick had acquired it. The quest to get it back had taken them to Cambodia where international gangsters were going to use the hand to gain supernatural powers. He and his wife had gotten out of that mess with their lives, but not the hand. But as a thank you for helping foil the gang's plan, their local contact had sent them some rubies from an old Cambodian mine. Rick had just cashed in those rubies for American greenbacks.

If there was one thing Rick understood, it was when you had a run of good luck, you needed to ride that wave. The delivery of a bag of rubies was one hell of a lucky event, and he wasn't about to let that luck run out without leveraging it.

So that night, he attended the weekly poker game that operated out of the back room of one of the Savannah bars. The players weren't the richest men in the city, but they were second-tier rich. Rick had wrangled an irregular invitation from Doug McAtee, the organizer, after they had made some profitable business deals. He and Rose had sold him a few fine antiques when Doug had been flush, and bought from him at a fair price when he hadn't been. Rick wasn't permitted to be a regular because he had an annoying tendency to win.

Tonight, the fifth man at the table was a newcomer, a young Englishman named Colin Farr. His passenger steamship had stopped overnight in Savannah and after being cooped up at sea for weeks, he'd decided to exploit the opportunity to enjoy time on dry land. And the man had been enjoying it. He'd been drinking before he started to play, and hadn't stopped as the game progressed. By now he was squinting at cards to tell what they were and the chips he tossed into the pot frequently missed the target. His stack of remaining chips was pretty small.

Rick knew better than to mix drinking and wagering. He'd mastered nursing one drink for an entire evening to stay clear-headed. Of course, sometimes he acted tipsy, to disarm the other players, but that was just part of the game. Half of playing poker was what went on beyond the cards in your hand.

Right now, the cards in his hand were good. Three queens and two eights were going to be tough to beat. The three regulars had folded as the price to stay in the hand got steeper. Now it was just down to him and Colin.

Colin had the wan complexion of a man who spent more time in London fog than seaside sunshine. High cheekbones accentuated his sallow cheeks and the part in his hair seemed to be as much combing as the dark, unruly mess could tolerate. His bleary eyes checked the cards in his hand far too many times for a man with a winning hand.

The bet was to Rick; a ten dollar raise. It looked like Colin was hoping he'd capitulate under the weight of the wager. Colin had hoped wrong.

Rick slid a stack of chips into the pot. "See your ten and raise you twenty."

Twenty dollars was all the visitor had left. Colin looked with distress at the paltry pile of chips at his seat. He slid his remaining chips in, then eyed the stack towering before Rick.

"I call your twenty," Colin said, "and raise you whatever you have left with this."

He unbuttoned his shirt and removed a gold chain from around his neck. At the end dangled an opal-cut, sapphire pendant so dark blue it was almost black. A golden Egyptian ankh symbol attached it to the chain. Colin held it suspended over the pot.

"This is worth more than what you have there," he said.

Rick gripped the chain between two fingers and held the sapphire up to the light. To the naked eye it seemed flawless. It was also over half an inch long. Even a sapphire half the size was worth more than what Rick had left to bet.

"Now, now," Doug said. The plump banker sat to Rick's left. "Table stakes rules, Mr. Farr. You can't bet more than you had at the table at the start of the hand. All you can do is call Mr. Sinclair's bet."

Rick considered his run of good luck and the price this sapphire would fetch when he sold it. "Technically, this little gem was 'at the table' when Colin sat down. I'm okay with bending the rules one time for our guest, if everyone else is."

The others at the table shrugged their indifference. Doug sighed. "Very well."

Colin smiled and dropped the sapphire into the pot. Rick slid in his remaining chips.

Colin grinned and showed his cards. Three jacks and two aces. "How do you like that hand?"

"A lot better than you'll like this one."

Rick laid down his queens and eights. Colin's jaw sagged.

"Should have stuck with table stakes, Mr. Farr," Doug said.

Rick picked up the sapphire from the pot and held it in his hand. The stone felt unbelievably cold. A sense of dread darkened his heart. He dropped the sapphire back onto the chips.

Rick took a deep breath and exhaled. The clock on the wall said it was well-past midnight. He'd been up for too many hours in a row and his mind was playing tricks on him about the sapphire. A rock was a rock.

There couldn't be anything supernatural about this stone.

CHAPTER THREE

The next morning, Rick came down from their apartment and entered the Treasure Hunters antique shop. He and Rose had run it for years and it had gotten them through this economic disaster people were rightly calling the Great Depression. They'd managed to buy low from the many people without money and then sell high to the few people who still did. They hadn't become one of those rich folks doing it, but they hadn't been too poor to eat, either.

The storefront shop contained rows of shelves filled with a wide variety of antiques displayed in a cluttered and haphazard manner. Rose was always after Rick to get it organized into categories. Rick thought it better if people had a discovery experience as they wandered through the shop. He also thought sorting through everything they had would bore him to tears.

Rose stood beside the cash register at the counter. He couldn't help but smile every time he saw her. Her red hair was pulled back in a ponytail which let all the room's light illuminate her porcelain complexion.

A stack of cash sat on the counter. She gave Rick a very serious look, then beckoned him over with her index finger.

There was ice in her blue eyes, and that was never a good sign.

He managed a sheepish grin and approached her.

"Imagine my surprise when I counted the cash drawer this morning," Rose said.

"Isn't it all there?" Rick said.

"Yes, it's all here. But in all the wrong denominations."

Rick realized that when the winnings had been divided up at night, he'd ended up with large bills.

"Simple explanation there. See, I made a temporary withdrawal from the cash register to do some investing."

Rose grimaced. "Were you investing in cards or horses?"

"I kept to a sound investment. Five card stud." Rick went to the other side of the counter, piled a wad of bills from a drawer there, and slapped them on the glass top. "And you'll be happy to know that investment paid dividends."

Rose slid the money over in front of her. "It's a good thing it did. We've just gotten our fiscal heads above water, and only barely. You shouldn't risk our working cash."

"Risk? When I'm playing? You must be thinking about someone else."

"No, I'm thinking of you specifically."

"With our score from the rubies," Rick said, "I knew we had a little financial breathing room, so I thought I'd let some of our cash get some air."

"Were you going to let me know about this 'dividend' at any point?"

"It was going to come to you in the form of roses this afternoon, but now you've gone and spoiled the surprise. That cost you a big smile."

"I'll smile even bigger making this month's mortgage payment early."

The bell on the shop door rang. Rick looked over and was surprised to see Colin. While he had cleaned up and put on fresh clothes, he certainly looked the worse for wear from his bender last night. He squinted against the light and moved deliberately, as if trying to keep his head perfectly level.

"Colin!" Rick said. When Rose looked confused about him knowing a stranger, he added, "Rose, this is Colin Farr from England. He was at last night's game."

"Nice to meet you," Rose said. "I hope that your part of the game's contribution to our coffers wasn't too great."

"Just what I'm here to discuss." He grabbed the counter for support. "I'm afraid I bet more than I could afford to lose last night."

"I don't know how they do it in England," Rick said, "but in America we don't refund betting losses."

Colin offered a dismissive wave of his hand. "Not the money, though that is also sorely missed. I mean the pendant."

Rose turned to Rick. "What pendant?"

Rick winced and then took a folded square of velvet from the same drawer he'd stashed the cash. He unfolded it to reveal the sapphire pendant. "Colin bet this on what turned out to be a losing hand. But in his defense, it was a very good losing hand."

"Yes, you see," Colin said, "it's a family heirloom, and I really must have it back."

"Lucky for you," Rick said, "we sell things here for a living. I think we can agree on a fair cash price."

"The problem there is you also have almost all my cash."

"You've made some poor decisions," Rick said, "I sympathize, because I've been there."

"I'll attest to that," Rose said.

Rick gave Rose an irked look and then turned back to Colin. "But a bet is a bet, and we need that cash as much as you do. There is a Depression going on."

Colin straightened up. "Sir, a gentleman does not welsh on his bets, and I'm not trying to do so. I'm offering payment for the pendant, though it would be payment in kind."

Rose rolled her eyes, but Rick was intrigued. "Go on."

"The pendant belonged to my grandmother, Florence Farr. She was an actress, quite famous in London's West End. She was also what they called back then a spiritualist, a member of a society called the Hermetic Order of the Golden Dawn."

Colin picked up the chain and let the pendant dangle. In the bright light of the shop, the sapphire was far more dazzling than in the darkened room where they'd been playing cards.

"This pendant was discovered in the tomb of Mut-em-menu, a high priestess of Sobekneferu, a female pharaoh of Ancient Egypt."

Rose's eyes widened. "I thought Cleopatra was the only female pharaoh."

"No, there were others, but their reigns were usually short. That was the case for Sobekneferu. She was deposed. She fled with a large amount of the royal coffers and was never found. Mut-em-menu travelled with her and outlived her. My grandmother claimed she could communicate with the old priestess through this pendant, and there were many credible reports of her being possessed by the priestess when she was in her trances."

"You had my full attention at the mention of missing royal coffers," Rick said.

"Now my grandmother claimed that Mut-em-menu could not rest until she directed someone to reunite this amulet with its twin on the body of her pharaoh, Sobekneferu. The reward would be the treasures within the tomb. But my grandmother died in 1917 before she could get to Egypt and discover the location."

Rose looked wary of this story. "So how did you end up with this pendant?"

"It passed first to my mother," Colin said. "But my mother was not only a disbeliever in such spiritualist things, she absolutely abhorred them. As a girl, she'd been on the receiving end of a lot of taunting and exclusion because of her mother's strange practices. When she inherited Grandmother's belongings, she refused to even unpack anything that had to do with the Hermetic Order of the Golden Dawn. After my father died in the Great War, she moved the two of us to British Guyana. She passed away last month."

"My condolences," Rose said.

Colin continued. "So, Mother kept that box of spiritualist items. Not sure if she was more afraid to open it or to throw it away. At any rate, after she passed, I did open it. Inside was the pendant and with the pendant was an address in Cairo and the date April 15, 1918."

"Any idea what's at that address?" Rick said.

"Absolutely. It's the address of the Hermetic Order of the Golden Dawn in Cairo. I believe that my grandmother had an appointment to pursue reuniting the pendant with the mummy, and then reaping the treasure of Sobekneferu. I want to follow through on her plan. That's why I was on my way to Cairo."

"A lot may have changed in thirty years," Rose said.

"I won't know until I get there," Colin said, "and I'll never know if I don't leave Savannah."

"So, you want me to give you back the pendant so you can finish this quest?" Rick said.

"That would hardly be fair. As I said, you won it on the up-and-up. I propose a partnership. We take the journey together, and split the proceeds of discovering the tomb. Say, 70-30?"

"With Rose and I being the 70?"

"No, that's my portion. See here, 70-30 is completely reasonable."

"Yet 60-40 is completely acceptable," Rick said.

Colin pondered the counter-proposal. "Given my circumstances, I am forced to agree to those terms."

Rose raised both hands in the air. "I'm not agreeing to those terms. Rick, no way you are running off to Egypt to talk with a mummy."

"This could have a great payout, Rosie. Colin, when does that steamship of yours leave port?"

"There's the rub. You see, it already has. I was forced to miss the departure in order to be here to retrieve the pendant. My ticket is forfeit, as is the money I paid for the passage."

"We'll have to buy tickets on the next available ship," Rick said.

"And here's the glue that cements our partnership," Colin said. "I haven't the funds to purchase passage, or much of anything else at the moment. For safety's sake, I only carried enough cash to get me to my destination, and that has been lost in a tragic poker-playing accident. The remainder of my inheritance is in the Bank of England, which has no branches here. But once we are in Egypt, I will have free access to those funds."

"So, you think we're buying you a ticket?" Rose said.

"Much more of a short-term loan, actually. You will be repaid after we disembark in Cairo and I get to a bank."

"I need to have a private discussion with my husband." Rose grabbed Rick's arm before he or Colin could respond. She dragged him from behind the counter and back to the storage and restoration room in the rear of the shop.

"You aren't considering this, are you?" she said.

Rick knew that the correct answer would have been no. And yet…

"This could be the chance for a big payout," he said.

"The person most susceptible to a con man is always a con man. Have you considered that this guy was broke and then worked himself into your card game to trick someone into buying him a ticket out of the country?"

"No one owning that sapphire is broke," Rick said, "and he brought money to the card table last night. And if he was scamming a ticket, why invite me along? Rosie, I know when someone's bluffing, and he isn't. If you don't think he's legit, come along and see. If he isn't, you can say I told you so. We can pick up some antiquities in Egypt we can resell here at a profit. You know how hot those kinds of things have been since those fellows found Tut's tomb."

"So now you want to add the expense of another steamship ticket to what we're investing?"

"No. With my plan, three can travel as cheaply as one. There are extra seats."

Rose gave him a shove in the chest. "If you're talking about flying with Humphrey in his death trap, forget it."

Humphrey Custis was Rick's friend from way back. He'd been a fighter ace in the Great War and now flew cargo around in his Ford Tri-motor airplane. Some of the cargo was even legal. Like the pilot, the plane had seen better days, but Humphrey had delivered Rick and Rose to a number of far-flung spots with only minor incidents.

"When he flew us to Cambodia," Rose continued, "we barely got there and back."

"For the record, 'barely' getting somewhere and getting somewhere are technically the same thing. And I know for a fact that Humphrey has been working on the plane since then and it is completely up-to-snuff."

Rick was more *hoping* Humphrey had been doing that than knowing it for a fact.

"Plus," Rick added, "you've always wanted to see the Pyramids and the Sphinx. When else will you get the chance? Colin will cover our expenses as soon as we land."

Rose tapped her jaw with her forefinger as she thought the idea through.

"Even when Colin comes up with nothing but desert sand," she said, "I should be able to bring back some interesting pieces. But I'm doing all the buying, and if after two days he hasn't gotten more than mumbo jumbo from the Hermetic Order, we fly home."

"Rosie, you have a deal. You won't regret it."

"Somehow, I always seem to."

Rick led her back out to the shop. Colin sat at the counter with a look of anticipation on his face.

"And?" he said.

"We're all going to Egypt," Rick said. "But all the expenses come out of your cut."

"Agreed. There will be so many riches that a fraction of it will still set me up for life."

Rick liked the sound of that.

CHAPTER FOUR

Later that day, as she drove back into Savannah, Rose felt a little better about this upcoming journey to Cairo.

She'd just finished speaking with Professor Bartholomew Keene at Martyn University. He taught classes in World History. He had always been a good source for background information during Rose's research about things in their shop.

With Egyptian history going back thousands of years, the professor had admitted that he couldn't recall any specifics about the female pharaoh Sobekneferu. He didn't teach any classes on Middle Eastern history.

However, he was able to give her the name of Dr. Mousa Khalifa as an excellent Cairo contact. The two of them had met at a conference and hit it off quite well. Rose was glad that once they arrived in Cairo, she'd be able to temper her husband's usual half-cocked enthusiasm with a little sober local insight.

She loved her husband dearly, and not just for his dashing good looks. (She wished no one had ever mentioned he resembled Errol Flynn and encouraged him to grow that pencil moustache he was now so proud of.) But he tended to be impulsive, especially around antique purchases. He'd frequently come home with a cheap oddity that likely had two potential buyers on the face of the Earth. Four out of five of them wouldn't sell, but he'd only remember that successful fifth one as he picked up the next screwball antique. The man lived to hit that longshot bet.

She was afraid that a longshot bet was what this Cairo trip would end up being. Rick was much more comfortable "looking before he leapt" than Rose was.

The idea of tracking down a lost burial treasure by speaking to the dead was crazy. So it was going to be up to her if they were going to return with enough collectibles to make the journey profitable.

Her next stop before home was the Savannah library. The beautiful building had been a fixture on Bull Street for decades. One of the few benefits of the Great Depression had been a WPA-funded expansion two years ago.

After a half hour inside the library, a search of the stacks had only yielded one slim, general overview of Egyptian history and one book about the discovery of the tomb of Tutankhamen in 1922. While this was better than nothing, it wasn't much better.

She dove into the overall history book first. The scope of the book was overwhelming.

Pharaonic rule seemed fraught with intrigue and power plays, both between and within families. A panoply of Egyptian gods was invoked to bless the rule of each and provide good weather and abundant crops. Egyptian civilization was among the most advanced at the time and included great cities and monuments, especially the kinds of pyramids that the country was now famous for. Each was a huge mausoleum for one pharaoh and the worldly goods the ruler thought he needed to bring with him into the afterlife.

Rose wondered how, if these things supposedly went with the pharaoh to the afterlife, looters found them still in tombs to be stolen.

Egyptian dynasties stretched back to 3150 BC and didn't come to an end until Roman incorporation during the time of Christ. Finding one pharaoh's reign in the book was going to be like finding a needle in a haystack. Thankfully, the index did give one page number as a reference for Sobekneferu.

All that page said was that she was the last pharaoh of the Twelfth Dynasty of the Middle Kingdom, about 4,000 years ago. A footnote noted that she was the first female pharaoh. She ascended to the throne following the death of Amenemhat IV, who was either her brother or husband, though her father had certainly been Amenemhat III. Her brief reign lasted under four years. Details about why and how she was succeeded weren't listed. Given the penchant for new rulers to erase the memories of the old, she could certainly see that happening to a female pharaoh.

That wasn't much information, but it confirmed that Sobekneferu had been a pharaoh so at least some of Colin's story was true. Given Sobekneferu's obscurity, if a London actress was faking some spiritualist connection, would it be to a priestess of that pharaoh? That seemed unlikely, but Rose wasn't about to take that as proof Colin's grandmother had been talking with the dead.

The next book about uncovering Tut's tomb proved to be much better reading.

After years of searching, Howard Carter, financed by George Herbert, Earl of Carnarvon, discovered the intact and un-pillaged tomb of Pharoah Tutankhamen in 1922. For the next seven years, Carter's team unearthed and conserved a collection of amazing treasures from art, to everyday articles, to the glorious golden sarcophagus of King Tut himself. Rose relished all the details about the discovery process and the meaning of the items found in the tomb. She also picked up a lot of details about the area and the people who live there.

The final chapter was pretty grim. It seemed that opening the tomb came with a price. Carnarvon died of a mysterious infection shortly after being in the tomb during its discovery. Captain Richard Bethell, Carter's private secretary, was found dead in a club in Mayfair in

1929. Then his father, Lord Westbury, jumped out of a window in his grief. Then a boy died who was knocked over by the Lord's hearse. There followed a long list of local workers stricken with strange ailments and fatal diseases.

Later, cartouches within the tomb were translated to warn of a curse upon any who entered and violated the peace of the pharaoh's afterlife. Carter lamented that he'd wished he'd known what those cartouches meant when excavation had begun.

Rose was ready to dismiss the idea of a mummy's curse out of hand as something only fit for one of those Universal Pictures monster movies. Evil curses were about as credible as Colin's grandmother communing with the dead. She wondered if the people in Egypt believed in all this superstitious nonsense.

CHAPTER FIVE

Rick piloted his motorcycle through the open gate of the abandoned Army airfield outside of Savannah. Rose hated when he rode his Indian motorcycle, but she had taken the truck on her research mission, so that had given Rick an excuse to take it out for a spin.

When he went to buy an estate two years ago, this 1923 Indian Scout had been leaning up against the side of a barn. Rick knew that behind the dry rotted tires, pounds of rust, and flayed seat cover, this motorcycle was a gem. He'd told the estate seller he'd have to throw it in for free. The seller agreed immediately.

He and Humphrey had gotten it back in running order. Well, mostly Humphrey, but Rick had provided moral support and handed him tools. Rose kept telling him he was going to kill himself riding it, but he assured her he was destined for a much more spectacular and heroic death.

This airfield had been active during the Great War, but both the downsized post-war military and the Depression-strapped local government had no interest in it now. That made it a perfect place for Humphrey to store his plane. The price was right (free) and the amount of scrutiny his departures and arrivals got was perfect (none at all.) These were important attributes when Humphrey ran some cargo that danced around the line of legality.

Humphrey's Tri-motor stood parked just south of the old control tower. Paint peeled off the tower's eastern side. Some of the tower's top windows were broken out and save for Humphrey living on the ground floor, nothing but pigeons had manned the tower in over a decade.

The boxy Tri-motor was the only girl at the dance so-to-speak. The aircraft sat alone beside the overgrown runway. She'd been named after the three-engine configuration, with one in the nose and one on each wing. The aircraft's exterior looked almost as abandoned as the runway, with faded tail numbers and a mildew-streaked cabin. But it was what was under the skin that mattered, and Humphrey kept the mechanicals in top-notch shape. Or at least that was what he said.

Rick found Humphrey sound asleep in a hammock set up under one wing. He wore his usual stained coveralls and an old Army service cap covered his face. No longer the dashing flyboy of years past, his belly stretched the coveralls to their limit. Rick crept up and stood by Humphrey's head.

"Oh, no!" he shouted. "It's the cops!"

Humphrey woke with such a start that he rolled out of his hammock and landed face-first on the ground. He was on his feet in a flash, holding his hat on his head with both hands. A few furtive looks around the airfield confirmed there were indeed no police officers present. Then his eyes settled on Rick and he relaxed.

"Aw, Ricky." Humphrey's Southern drawl was thick. "What did you have to go and do that for? I was in the middle of a beautiful dream."

"I'm replacing your sleeping dream with a dream trip," Rick said. "We're going to Cairo."

"What's in Illinois?"

"Not Cairo, Illinois. Cairo, Egypt."

Humphrey raised an eyebrow. "Egypt like the other side of the world Egypt?"

"That's the one. How soon can you be ready?"

Humphrey scratched his head under his cap. "Gotta do a pretty thorough pre-flight for a trip like that, check the charts for a course, load up some spares and other gear. Probably tomorrow morning."

"Dawn it is then!"

"Maybe a little less morning than that. And you're gonna need to co-pilot in the cockpit and navigate."

Rick was no certified pilot, but Humphrey had taught him enough to take over some of the secondary duties. "Roger that."

"And not like our last trip where you only pretended to know where we were on the map."

"My friend, I'm wounded that you would think that."

"You was holding the map upside down."

Rick waved off his concerns. "Have no fear. I'll be the perfect co-pilot."

"How come we're going to Egypt?"

"We're taking a Brit over to help him find the lost treasure of an Egyptian pharaoh. Then we'll be splitting the proceeds, with the lion's share going to us."

"I could use some of that lion's share. War jitters in Europe has got the import market confused as goats in a henhouse. Work's been a mite hard to come by."

"We'll make so much you'll be able to buy a new plane."

"As if I'd want to." Humphrey gave the Tri-motor a thump on the side. "Solid as a rock. Say, we'll need to get some money fronted to fuel the plane up."

Rick cringed. "Can't help you there. You'll have to figure that part out. But I promise we'll repay your expenses right off the top, before we divide up the spoils."

Humphrey looked leery. "Gee, Rick, gas ain't free, you know."

Rick clapped him on the shoulder. "You're a veteran scrounger. Nothing you can't handle. I'll have the three of us and our baggage here in the morning and the next stop will be the pyramids of Egypt."

"Actually, we'll first be stopping in Bermuda, then…"

"Details, details," Rick said. "Just make sure you have a safe place around here to store all the riches we'll come back with."

Humphrey smiled. "Sure thing, Rick."

Rick went back to his motorcycle and fired it up. With transportation arranged, his part of the planning process was complete. Once they got there, Colin would lead them to the pharaoh's tomb.

He hoped.

CHAPTER SIX

Two days later

As they finally approached Cairo for landing, the size of the city shocked Rose. What it lacked in skyscraper height, it more than made up for in breadth. Cairo stretched out for miles along the eastern bank of the Nile River and then out past what the haze made visible. The minarets of many mosques created what little skyline there was. Above it all perched the massive domes and castle-like walls of the Citadel of Saladin. The tourist guide Rose had devoured said that it had been built in Medieval times and had once been the seat of government. While it had been listed as a "must see" attraction, Rose doubted they would have time for sightseeing, which was kind of a shame.

The Tri-motor touched down at a small, sandy airstrip at the city's edge. The plane rolled to a stop. Rose looked out the window and was underwhelmed. There was no control tower, just a few shacks. Mule-drawn carts and laden camels trod along the road at the airfield's edge.

Colin sat in the seat in front of Rose. She tapped his shoulder. "Doesn't Cairo have a real airport?"

"Yes," he said, "quite a nice one, in fact. This one is much better for a more private arrival."

Rose translated *private* as *illegal*. This was not how she wanted this excursion to begin. She looked at the passports she held in her hand, grumbled, and tossed them back in her bag. She guessed they would not be necessary.

Rick and Humphrey came back from the cockpit. Rick was all smiles. Humphrey looked dog-tired and Rose knew he'd been doing all the work up there.

"Welcome to Cairo, Rosie!" Rick said.

She ignored him and looked at Humphrey. "You call this an airport?"

"Sure is. I've used it before."

Rose rolled her eyes. "Swell. My worst fears were just confirmed."

The desert sun had already driven the cabin to an oven-like temperature. Colin scrambled back to the door and threw it open. A blast of hot wind coated the cabin floor in a fine, yellow sand. He folded down the steps.

"First things first," Colin said. "I have to meet the contact given to me by the Hermetic Order of the Golden Dawn. That's step one to finding the tomb."

"Actually, before that we need to go to your bank," Rick said, "so we can finance this trip."

"Yes." Colin flashed a less than genuine smile. "Quite right."

"I have a contact Professor Keene gave me for help understanding the area and antiquities," Rose said. "That would be the best place to start."

"Y'all," Humphrey said. "I'm more inclined to a long shower and a long sleep in a soft bed as stop number one."

"All splendid points," Colin said. "We shall do them all simultaneously with the help of a local dragoman."

"A what?" Rick said.

"A certified guide and interpreter," Rose said. "Didn't you read that tourist guide I gave you?"

"Selected highlights," Rick said.

"Meaning the section on cabarets and casinos."

"It was so well-written, I couldn't turn the next page."

Rose looked out at the desolate airfield. "Will we find a dragoman here?"

"Oh, no," Colin said. "Rest assured that they will find us."

The group grabbed their bags and left the plane, which Humphrey then triple locked. That confirmed Rose's assessment about the kind of airfield this was. Just as Colin had predicted, at the entrance to the airfield four men with mule-drawn carts stood there with eager looks on their faces. They wore long, silk robes and tight, high caps. One wore a black fez and had a large black-and-white checked scarf wrapped around his neck.

They looked like they were ready to sprint for the baggage-laden travelers. The man in the black fez stepped forward first, turned and gave a bellicose set of commands in Arabic to the others. The other three looked fearful and took a step back. The man in the black fez wheeled around and approached the group. He smiled and displayed a mouth full of rotting teeth.

"I am Donkor Nisam," he said with both arms outstretched. "Your humble dragoman at your service for the duration of your visit to enchanted Egypt."

Colin gave him the once-over. "You know your way around the city?"

"Yes, most certainly. My family has been here for hundreds of years. In the tradition of their service to the pharaohs, I now happily serve you." He pointed to a wagon with a scruffy looking donkey in harness to it. "Come. We go right away."

Colin spent a split-second in consideration. "All right then. Here we go."

Rose grabbed Rick's arm and put her lips to his ear. "Don't you think we ought to shop around? I don't like how Donkor bullied those other three. And they didn't give me the willies like he does."

Rick patronizingly patted her hand. "Aw, Rosie, that's the kind of guide we want. A strong one who will make sure we get where we need to go, someone who has some authority. And if he passes muster with Colin, he must be all right."

Rose didn't fully trust Colin, so she wasn't about to trust someone based on Colin's dubious standards. She turned to Humphrey for some support.

Humphrey was half-asleep on his feet. She could tell he'd agree to anything that might get him closer to a bed.

"Rick, when hiring this dragoman turns everything upside down, you're never going to hear the end of it."

"And to prove I'm the bigger person," Rick said, "when we're filthy rich from the pharaoh's treasure, I'm not going to bring up how misplaced your reservations were. Well, I won't bring it up often."

The four took seats in a wagon that even Rose's grandparents would have considered substandard. Rose gave Donkor the address of Dr Mousa Khalifa and Colin gave him an address for the Hermetic Order of the Golden Dawn. Donkor took the front seat and snapped the reins. The donkey began a reluctant journey into the city.

Rose was soon pleasantly surprised by what she saw. The city center looked almost Parisian, with wide streets, modern buildings, streetcars, and automobiles. Nowhere near as many cars as Savannah or other American cities, but given the fact that she was travelling in a donkey-driven cart, she hadn't expected to see any.

Donkor looked over to her. "You look shocked, Madame."

Rose was embarrassed that her face had betrayed her. "Well, yes. This isn't the picture Americans have of Cairo."

"You can thank Napoleon," Donkor said. "He thought we should be a Paris-on-the-Nile and rebuilt our humble city in that image. It is quite popular with Europeans."

"And with the locals?"

"Most cannot afford the type of business transacted here."

They soon passed a four-story stone hotel as long as a city block. It boasted a soaring entrance and a wide patio with al fresco dining in front. The sign that arced over the entrance read *Shepheard's Hotel*. The people seated outside and clientele passing through the front door were dressed in the height of fashion.

Rose wasn't going to waste time asking if Colin had reserved them rooms there.

A few blocks further down, Donkor stopped in front of a three-story apartment building that would have been right at home in any European city. Rose's address was on the first floor. Dr. Khalifa had assured Professor Keene that he would be home the day Rose arrived.

"I will take the others to the second address," Donkor said, "and be back here in one hour."

"That okay with you, Rosie?" Rick said.

Rose glanced around the neighborhood and it seemed safe, at least much safer than the area around the airfield. "I should be fine."

Rose left the wagon and proceeded up the steps to the apartment building. The people on the street gave her strange looks. She realized what a sight she must have been after hours of travel and being delivered by donkey wagon.

She entered the building, found the right apartment, and knocked on the door.

She hoped Dr. Khalifa could fill in the details she needed to know.

CHAPTER SEVEN

As the cart pulled away from the building, Humphrey turned to Rick. “You okay with leaving Miss Rose all by her lonesome in Cairo?”

Rick was having serious second thoughts about it. “Well, this looks like a high-end neighborhood, and this Dr. Khalifa was recommended by someone she trusts.”

“As long as that’s enough to put your mind at ease, that’s swell.”

But it really wasn’t. As the cart rolled down the street, Rick kept an eye on the apartment door until he saw Rose step inside.

Minutes later, Donkor stopped them in front of a branch of the Anglo Egyptian Bank. The Union Jack flapped at the flagstaff protruding from the building. The stone edifice, heavy wooden doors, and even the twin gas lamps that flanked them were all in classic British style. Rick guessed that made the British feel much safer having their savings in there.

Rick turned to Colin. “Well?”

“Yes, right. In I go.”

Colin hopped out of the wagon and trotted up the few steps to the door. A British Army officer exited just as he arrived and held the door for him.

A few minutes later, Colin exited the bank. The grim look on his face was not reassuring. He climbed back into the wagon without a word. Humphrey had fallen asleep sitting up.

“Any trouble?” Rick said.

“Not a bit. I was able to withdraw everything in the account.”

"Shouldn't that mean you need a suitcase? But seriously, where's the money?"

"Right here." Colin patted the front pocket of his pants and sighed. "One hundred and twelve pounds sterling."

Rick's face fell. "You're joking."

"I wish I were. I'm embarrassed to admit that that was the full sum in the account."

"What happened to the rest of it?"

Colin winced. "Afraid that's all there ever was."

"You flat out lied to us?"

"If you'd known my sad pecuniary state," Colin said, "you would have never made the passage to Egypt."

Rick felt his face get red. "If I'd known you didn't have enough money to pay our way home? Hell, no we wouldn't have flown here."

"This is all quite salvageable," Colin said. "The treasure shall make us instantly wealthier than you could imagine."

"I have a very good imagination," Rick said.

"The Hermetic Order will be bound by our code to get us on our feet. They will believe in our quest for the treasure and be happy to give us the bit of support we need to find it. All of this will work out."

Colin played poker poorly, and was playing this game of juggling his stories even worse. A novice card player could spot a bluff this awful.

"Donkor," Rick said, "take us to our next address."

Donkor turned around and sent the donkey in motion with a snap of the reins. With the dragoman engaged in getting them through the streets, Rick turned back to Colin.

"Give the money to me," Rick whispered to him.

"Why should I do that?" he answered in an offended, hushed tone.

"Because at this point, I don't trust you as far as I can throw you. I wouldn't put it past you to wander off with that paltry purse and leave us stranded. I'll feel much more comfortable holding what little money we have."

"You already have the amulet."

"And in this game, it's best if I hold all the cards. At least for now. Now hand it over while Donkor isn't looking."

Colin reluctantly reached into his pocket and pulled out a slim wad of banknotes. He gave them to Rick and Rick buried them deep in his pocket.

Donkor drove the cart into an older section of Cairo. Here the buildings were much smaller, much older, and much closer together. The streets narrowed and went from pavement to sand. Cars disappeared as did any Western clothing. The men all wore the kind of traditional long robe Donkor wore and a variety of head coverings. Most of the men eyed Rick with distrust, and the rest with open antipathy.

Another change was that the crowd became almost exclusively male. The few women he saw were dressed in flowing black from head to toe, with a veil that left only their eyes exposed.

He could only imagine Rose's violent reaction to having to dress like that.

Donkor stopped the cart before a narrow, nondescript single family home. It was wedged between two others and had two stories, with an unsafe-looking balcony on the second floor. A tabby cat sat on the balcony railing and peered down at them with only mild interest.

"Are you quite sure this is the address?" Colin asked.

"This is the address you gave me," Donkor said.

Rick shook Humphrey awake, and then the three of them climbed out of the cart. They took their bags and Rick took Rose's. As they knocked on the door, Donkor set the cart rolling, Rick guessed to go back and pick up Rose. He thought Donkor might have waited to see if someone answered the door. Colin seemed unfazed by the neighborhood, but Rick sure didn't want to be left on the street alone.

He breathed a sigh of relief when the door opened. A short, older woman in an awful brunette wig gave them a quizzical look. She was plump and with her Western housecoat would have looked right at home gardening behind an English flat. She scowled at the three of them.

"Alice Meriwether?" Colin extended his hand. "I'm Colin Farr."

The woman's scowl deepened.

"Grandson to Florence Farr," Colin added.

The woman's face brightened. She shook Colin's hand. "Dear Florence! Well, what a surprise."

Now it was Rick's turn to scowl. Apparently, Colin hadn't made any arrangements for this meeting with the Hermetic Order. Lie Number Two from Colin revealed.

"My partners in this adventure," Colin said, "Humphrey Custis and Rick Sinclair."

Humphrey responded with a sleepy nod.

"How do you do?" Rick said. "My wife Rose will be joining us shortly."

"Do come in!" Alice said.

The three stepped in. The place looked more like a warehouse than a home. The rooms were crammed with Egyptian items. Paintings leaned against walls. Mismatched chairs were stacked one inside another. Weathered wooden boards festooned with cartouches hung from walls. Figurines of Egyptian gods, pharaohs, and a variety of animals crowded shelves and tables. Overhead, a dusty ceiling fan spun in a lazy, useless circle. If the place hadn't been so dirty and disorganized, it might have passed for one of the curio shops in the newer part of the city.

But the real shocker was the smell. The oppressive stink of cat urine fogged the air, and the source was readily apparent. Rick could count six cats from where he stood, a variety of breeds, each sprawled out on any space uncluttered enough to support it. A few more prowled the floor. One sleek, jet-black feline sat atop a curio cabinet surveying the scene as if it was a pharaoh. It looked most closely at the three visitors.

"Luckily," Alice said, "I had just straightened up some of my collection this morning."

Rick and Humphrey exchanged shocked looks, wondering what the heck this place looked like before she "straightened" it.

"Y'all got a lot of cats," Humphrey said.

"Ah yes, it is the Egyptian way."

Rick doubted that every house in the city looked like a cage-free pet shop.

"The ancient Egyptians held cats in a special reverence," Alice said, "appreciating their beauty, grace, and special connection to the gods. They mummified cats along with the pharaohs."

Rick guessed those "revered" cats weren't allowed to die of old age before the process.

The old lady teetered back to a table and chairs. The table was about the only uncluttered space in the room. She pulled out a chair and a sleeping Siamese cat exploded out of the seat. Alice took its place.

"Your grandmother had always said she would visit," Alice said, "but that never came to be."

"The war put a stop to travel," Colin said, "and she passed on before peace made the passage possible again."

"So, unlike your mother, you have embraced your grandmother's experiences?"

"I'm certainly more open to accepting them," he said. "My mother's resentment about Grandmother's lifestyle may have had her instinctively oppose my grandmother's beliefs."

"If I remember right," Alice said, "Florence had an amulet."

Colin looked to Rick. Rick pulled the amulet up from under his shirt, released the clasp of its chain, and then held it by the chain in front of Alice.

"She was certain this amulet was linked to the spirit of Mut-em-menu," Colin said, "and would lead us to the tomb of her pharaoh, Sobekneferu."

Alice caressed the amulet with one finger. "Has the priestess spoken to you through this amulet?"

"Well, no," Colin said.

"Then we will have to use the summoning ritual to open that doorway," Alice said.

Rick looped the amulet chain back over his head. "What's a summoning ritual?"

"An ancient ritual from the Egyptian *Book of the Dead* that can bring spirits from the Netherworld back into ours."

"Talking with the dead, now that's a mite hard to believe," Humphrey said. "It's 1938, not 1638."

"You will believe after participating in the summoning ritual," Alice said. "You most surely will. Please be seated."

"Whoa," Rick said, "we're in no shape for anything but sleep. We've been travelling forever and our bodies are on American time."

"Yeah," Humphrey added, 'I could use some shut-eye."

"I understand," Alice said. "Where are you staying?"

Rick looked at Colin as his third lie was laid bare before the world. He'd said the Hermetic Order had arranged for lodgings. Colin looked sheepish.

"Alice, I was hoping you could help us with that," Colin said.

"You said you had cabled the Hermetic Order in England," Rick said, "and they'd made arrangements for lodgings."

"I definitely did the former," Colin said. "Sadly, the Order hadn't agreed to the latter."

The gravity of Colin's cumulative lies and half-truths fully weighed on Rick. Rose was going to bury him in a swarm of I-told-you-so's. They were now on the other side of the globe with nowhere to stay, no money, and no local connections except a possibly crazy woman who thought she could talk with the dead.

He sure hoped that Rose was uncovering something much more useful.

CHAPTER EIGHT

Rose took a deep breath. They had a lot riding on Dr. Khalifa being as helpful as Professor Keene had promised. She knocked on the doctor's apartment door.

The door opened and revealed a slight old man with just a fringe of silver hair. A pair of round glasses perched on the end of his oversized nose. He wore a modern, European-style shirt and pants.

"Dr. Khalifa? I'm Rose Sinclair."

The man's face brightened. "Ah, yes. I've been expecting you. Please come in."

In the style she expected of every college professor, the apartment was modestly furnished with a rather utilitarian table and chairs. A set of open windows gave a view of the avenue and a welcome breeze fluttered the thin, open curtains. Bookshelves covered the rest of the wall space. They took seats at the table.

"Professor Keene cabled and asked me to help with your understanding of Egypt and our local customs," he said. "He was so kind to me during the conference we attended that I said I'd be delighted to help. What brings you to Cairo?"

Rose wasn't about to blurt out that they were in search of a lost tomb. "My husband and I run an antiques store in Savannah. We thought we'd bring back some Egyptian pieces for some of our regular clients."

"Very good. But first, you must be careful to understand the true provenance of what you are buying. Some artisans can make modern fakes look hundreds of years old. Second, there are severe export restrictions for Egyptian antiquities. Since Roman times, foreigners have pillaged our history. Now there are laws to prevent that. Excavations are closely monitored by the government."

Rose could see how those laws were going to run headlong into Rick and Colin's finders-keepers plan for the treasures of the lost pharaoh.

"If you are buying from a legitimate dealer," Dr. Khalifa continued, "you will have nothing to worry about."

"I'll assume one of the local dragomen can recommend a local dealer," she said.

Dr. Khalifa spat on the floor. "Dragomen! A once honorable profession that's now a refuge for charlatans and thieves. They lie about their expenses, they lie about their family lines, they even lie about their lies. Perhaps you can trust one recommended by Shepheard's Hotel, but I would not trust the rest any more than I would trust a cobra."

The professor just validated all Rose's misgivings about Donkor. But instead of feeling vindicated, she felt afraid for Rick and the others.

"Forgive me," the professor said. "I went straight into teaching without any hospitality. Let me get you some tea."

"Thank you."

The break was fine with Rose. Dr. Khalifa had just delivered a stream of information that felt like it came from a fire hose. And the worst part was, almost all of it was bad.

Moments later, Dr. Khalifa returned with two steaming, clear glasses of light-colored tea.

"This is Koshary Shai, my favorite tea. I prepare it with mint and sugar."

Rose took the glass and sipped. It was quite good and, with the mint and sugar flavors, it was practically a dessert. She complimented Dr. Khalifa on the beverage.

"American history goes back less than two hundred years," she said. "Egyptian history goes back for thousands."

"Yes. Teaching our nation's history cannot be completed in one semester, or even two."

"When I was reading up on it, I was intrigued to see there was a female pharaoh named Sobekneferu, but that was about all the information I could find."

Dr. Khalifa shook his head. "Even our own histories say little about the Queen of the Crocodiles."

"That's a name I hadn't seen for her."

"When her husband the pharaoh died, she claimed the throne because her father had been pharaoh previously. This was not how succession was supposed to go, and it was certainly not supposed to elevate a female to be ruler of the land. Yet, in spite of the vast power of the entrenched state against her, she rose to rule. The mysterious deaths of her enemies were attributed to her use of ancient, primeval magic.

"Once in power, the source of that magic became clear. She had unlocked the secrets of the *Book of the Dead*."

"That sounds ominous," Rose said.

"Oh, it is. The book held the rituals for passing in and out of the Underworld, for communicating with the gods, for access to dark magical power. So dangerous was this book that a later pharaoh's edict ordered every copy destroyed."

"So, none survived?"

"There are always rumors that a copy has been discovered, or surviving fragments have been unearthed. It is best if neither of those things ever happen. Such black magic cannot be controlled."

"What did Sobekneferu do with this power?" Rose said.

"She moved the seat of government south to a location by Lake Moeris. The course of the Nile that fed it has long since shifted and now it is a much-diminished oasis named Birket Quran. There she built a lavish complex and labyrinth called Crocodopolis. This was normal for a pharaoh to do, but she dedicated it to the god Sobek, and that was not normal."

"Who was Sobek?"

"Sobek was an ancient god, one with the head of a crocodile and the body of a man. In the mythology, there was a fight between two brother gods, Osiris and Seth. Seth murdered his brother, chopped his body into pieces, and threw them into the Nile. In an awful act of sacrilege, the crocodile-headed god devoured those body parts. The council of Egyptian gods tried him. Sobek was found guilty and punished. The story goes on to say that Sobek's punishment was to be imprisoned with his tongue cut off. Sobek was to be forever on the dark and disgraced side of the god's pantheon."

"Until Sobekneferu brought him in for a sequel."

"He offered her his power and support in return for her making him the true god of Egypt," Dr. Khalifa said, "and give him the chance to enact revenge on the other gods."

"We're sure this city she built wasn't just another myth?"

"The labyrinth temple, dubbed Crocodopolis, was described in detail by the historian Herodotus, who visited it. Thousands of rooms, some flooded and some not, housed hundreds of crocodiles. Unwilling human beings were sacrificed there, all building up to freeing Sobek and allowing a reunion with his tongue. Then he could cast the spells to imprison the gods who once punished him."

"I read that Sobekneferu only ruled for four years or so."

"True. Her gender, her illegitimate rise to the throne, and above all, her elevation of an evil god were more than the ruling class could bear. Before she could complete the final ceremonies to heal Sobek at Crocodopolis, the military deposed her while she was in Alexandria. Her magic allowed her and a few bodyguards to slip away, but the rest of the royal household was executed."

Rose figured the priestess Mut-em-menu had been killed in that coup, hence her spirit driving the search for Sobekneferu through the twin amulets.

But this story didn't mesh with Colin's tale of the pharaoh being buried with her treasure. Royalty on the run weren't going to be escaping with their coffers intact, or even be properly mummified and interred when captured by the rebels.

If she and Rick did find the pharaoh, but with nothing of value, affording to get back home was going to be a problem.

"Sobekneferu's party was later surrounded on the way to Crocodopolis," Dr. Khalifa continued. "The pharaoh was killed and buried somewhere in the desert. Then the army marched on Crocodopolis. There the magic of Sobek protected it with dangerous weather and savage animal attacks. The story goes that the high priests invoked the intercessions of Horus and others. Those gods had the ground swallow the entire city, then had a sandstorm wipe clean any trace from the surface of the Earth. All within were buried alive."

"Has Crocodopolis ever been found?" she said.

"No. A British tomb robber named Petrie claimed to have found it in 1912, but all he really found was a small temple dedicated to Sobek. It was from the right time period, but nowhere near large enough to have been the labyrinth of Crocodopolis. No Egyptian in their right mind wants to find that city."

"You are kidding, right?"

"Certainly not. We take our past tales seriously. Sobek was the personification of evil. There was a reason the powerful in Egypt rose up and destroyed Crocodopolis. They saw it as a threat not just to Egypt, but to the world."

Rose knew better than to take local myths at face value. But she also knew they could not be dismissed out of hand. Stories like these tales of Sobek always had some kernel of truth at their center.

She was afraid that this kernel might be big enough to make finding the tomb of Sobekneferu very dangerous.

CHAPTER NINE

As he stood in Alice's living room with the others, Rick's heart sank over Colin's failure to get them somewhere to stay.

"Oh my," Alice said. "There are no lodgings around here, and the hotels in the city are frightfully expensive, as well as often completely booked this time of year."

Rick turned to Colin, ready to give him hell for all the lies he'd spun about this trip.

"Ma'am, we're at the 'any port in a storm' stage of things here," Humphrey said. He added a yawn for emphasis.

Just then, a knock sounded at the door. Alice opened the door to reveal Rose with Donkor standing behind her. They entered and Rick made introductions. Rose gave the cluttered house a sidelong look that Rick knew meant stifled disapproval.

"Well," Alice said, "since everyone is here, I must make you all tea. Please be seated and I'll be right back."

She scurried off to the rear of the house. Rose took a self-guided tour of the disorganized collection in the room. The others gathered around the table.

Rick got his first good look at it. The inlay on the top looked a bit like one of the pie-type wheels spun at carnivals to award prizes. But each slice of the pie had a variety of Egyptian cartouches in it and the top of each slice contained what he guessed were Egyptian gods, mostly men with the heads of a variety of animals. While the cats seemed willing to lounge in every available open space, none ventured onto the table.

"Donkor," Colin began, "I might need to tap your local expertise. We are in need of suitable lodgings."

Rose gave Rick a furious look. "We don't have a place to stay?"

"And that's not the worst of it," Rick said.

Donkor shook his head. "The Western hotels are very expensive and are certainly full this time of year."

"So I've heard," Rick said.

"I may know of a place nearby. You will be safe there. I will go check."

"I just hope it's quiet," Humphrey said.

Donkor departed.

"This woman is the expert from the Hermetic Order of the Golden Dawn?" Rose said.

"Yes," Colin said.

"Well, I don't know what she knows about Egyptian mythology, but she doesn't know anything about antiques. This is the worst collection of fakes ever. They only *look* dirty and old."

"Are you sure?" Rick said.

Rose picked up a clay tablet containing Egyptian cartouches. She showed Rick the edge where the contemporary pigment had scraped away to reveal a gray base color. "Yes, I'm sure."

Alice returned with a very British tea set. She shooed away a cat and set it on an end table. Rick thought it odd she did not use the table they stood around.

"You have been collecting Egyptian artifacts long?" Rose asked.

"Oh, yes," Alice said. "The Hermetic Order of the Golden Dawn took up donations to send me here years ago so I could create some direct connections to this wonderful land and to continue to do research. I was lucky that so many local vendors offered me so many wonderful artifacts."

"Lucky indeed," Rose said.

Alice handed out cups of tea. "Each artifact was so unique, I couldn't seem to say no. Now I'm quite overrun with them. I've sent several back to the Order in England."

"And they appreciate them?" Rose said.

"Oh, they positively gush over them!"

Donkor stepped back through the front door. "I have secured lodgings for all of you, whenever you are ready."

Humphrey practically dropped his tea cup back on the tray. "I was ready an hour ago."

"Thank you for your hospitality, Alice," Rick said. "We'll be back in the morning for the summoning ritual."

"That will be splendid! See you on the morrow."

All returned their cups to the tray and took their bags back out to the wagon. The donkey pulled them down a few blocks and stopped in front of a bakery selling flat bread and a variety of other baked goods Rick didn't recognize. Donkor led them to carry their luggage up a set of steps on the outside of the building to the second floor. The door opened to a sparsely furnished room with a sink and stove in one corner. Doors opened to two adjoining bedrooms. A set of tall glass doors opened to a balcony.

"The baker beneath us is a friend," Donkor said. "He and the family used to live here before they could afford a house. He is happy to loan it to us while you stay. He asks for a third of the price of a Western hotel."

"We'll take it," Humphrey said.

He headed straight for one of the bedrooms and collapsed into the bed. Snoring followed almost immediately.

Rick pulled out a few pieces of currency from the wad in his pocket. He counted out the fee, gave it to Donkor, and returned the remainder. He saw Rose was about to ask him why he had money all of a sudden.

With a sharp shake of his head, he preempted her question. She nodded in understanding.

"I will be back to take you over to Alice's home in the morning," Donkor said. "And then wherever the spirits direct you."

Donkor left and closed the door behind him.

"I'll be quite comfortable out here," Colin said, "leaving you two the other bedroom."

Rick wanted to dope slap Colin for trying to sound magnanimous. Given the situation his lies had gotten them into, he was lucky Rick wasn't making him sleep outside. He and Rose went to the bedroom and closed the door behind them. The small bed looked old but serviceable, though the thin excuse for a mattress was supported by a mesh of rope. Rick and Rose sat on the edge.

"Okay," Rose said in a hushed tone. "Why do you have money, and why don't we have a hotel?"

Rick gave her a brief synopsis of Colin's multiple deceits. Rose rolled her eyes as the story kept getting worse.

She then relayed what she'd learned about Egypt and the first female pharaoh. Then Rose talked about all the export restrictions on artifacts. Rick didn't like the sound of that at all. She finished with direct quotes from Dr. Khalifa about not trusting dragomen.

"I don't know," Rick said. "Donkor seems on the up-and-up. He's gotten us around and if it wasn't for him, we'd have nowhere to stay."

Rose looked around the room. "Well, while it is the definition of 'better than nothing,' I'm grateful for it."

Rick gave Rose a hug. "We had a few bumps in the road, but starting in the morning, everything will be smooth sailing. Trust me."

CHAPTER TEN

As Donkor drove them back to Alice's house the next morning, Rose was feeling better about their situation. A good night's sleep helped a lot, and Donkor brought some Egyptian bread and cheese for breakfast. He refused Rick's offer of payment and said all that would be taken care of at trip's end. Rose remembered Dr. Khalifa saying that dragomen overcharged for everything, but was fine with keeping as much of their minimal cash in Rick's pocket as possible.

"Ricky," Humphrey said, "I don't know why I need to be coming to this here magic show. I could have stayed back and got in a little more shut-eye. And I could have been watchdog over our stuff."

"I assure you that that apartment is quite secure," Donkor said.

"And we need you with us," Rick said. "We all stick together from here on in."

"Don't put no stock in this séance mumbo jumbo no-how," Humphrey said.

"Oh, you will," Colin said. "The Hermetic Order are expert practitioners of the lost arts of Ancient Egypt. The knowledge of the rituals has been passed down from generation to generation stretching back to the time of the pharaohs."

"My mama used to tell me stories of Greek myths," Humphrey said. "Didn't mean none of them was true."

Soon they were back at Alice's home. Donkor waited outside with the cart as they entered. The house still smelled of cat when they entered, but now it was mingled with the aroma of incense. This wasn't the pleasant scent Rose associated with some of the Catholic churches at home or the homey smell of a fireplace. This incense had a harsh, bitter odor, and it had left behind a haze as if a room of people had been smoking the world's cheapest cigarettes.

Alice practically danced as she approached the group. "Welcome! I've already cleansed the room with special incense."

Humphrey leaned over to Rick. "The Meuse-Argonne battlefield smelled better than this."

"Come join me at the table," Alice said.

Everyone headed to the table. There were four seats. Alice pulled one out and again sent the same Siamese cat bolting from the seat and into the next room. That left them one short for everyone to sit down.

Humphrey stopped and leaned against the wall. 'You're a little short on seating there, so I'll just watch from here."

"You'll miss the experience," Alice said.

"I'll suffer the loss, ma'am," Humphrey said.

Four candles burned in the center of the table arranged around the falcon-headed Egyptian god picture there. Rose recognized it as Horus, god of kingship, the sun, and the sky. Other gods were depicted around the table's edge. The god she did not see was the crocodile-headed Sobek.

"Your grandmother was in contact with Mut-em-menu," Alice said, "and you wish to speak to the priestess?"

"Yes," Colin said. "And we brought the amulet Grandmother used to make her connection."

Rick took the amulet from his pocket, held it by the chain, and let it dangle over the table.

"The connection will be stronger," Alice said, "if it goes through the blood relative of the one contacted before."

Rick shrugged and handed the amulet to Colin. Colin placed the chain around his neck and the amulet lay flat against his chest.

"Now often the results of my incantations are very subtle," Alice said. "Sometimes others see nothing, but I can feel the spirit's presence and will describe it."

Rose sensed a charlatan. She gave Rick a look that said just that. In return, he managed a weak smile.

Alice placed a silver plate in the center of the table containing what looked like bits of parchment.

"These snippets are bindings from a mummy of the same dynasty as Sobekneferu," Alice said. "Treated and enchanted in the same way as hers. As they burn, they will help open a doorway to the afterlife of those who passed on at that time."

Alice began a chant that had an Arabic sound to it but at the same time was no language Rose had ever heard before. After a few bars, Alice paused, lit a match, and dropped it in the silver plate. The binding scraps caught fire in an instant.

Alice intoned several more chants. The air in the room turned heavy and oppressive.

The yellow flames in the plate turned a turquoise blue. Smoke that same color spread out from the dish like a fog, covered the table, then flowed over the edge. The three cats still hanging around screeched like someone had stepped on their tails and bolted from the room.

Rose gasped.

"Well, I'll be," Humphrey whispered as he stepped forward and stood behind Rick and Rose's chairs.

"Oh, my," Alice said. Her success at this pseudo-séance seemed to shock her.

"Mut-em-menu," she continued in a voice far shakier than the one she'd used chanting. "We call on you to guide us to the resting place of your pharaoh Sobekneferu."

The amulet around Colin's neck rose and floated before his chest. The stone in the center glowed bright blue. It swiveled to the left and pointed at the wall.

"It's tugging at my neck," Colin said. "As if it's pointing the way."

Alice gasped and fanned herself with one hand. "Well, this is certainly more than—"

Suddenly she shot to her feet and flipped her chair backward behind her. Her eyes rolled up into her head leaving only the whites. Her face seemed to transform into someone else's, an old woman, though one whose age could not erase the natural beauty of her youth.

Colin gasped.

Alice's face contorted in fury. She turned to Colin.

"Mut-em-menu will kill you if you fail." Alice's voice was so different that it seemed she could not have affected it. It was raspy and in a frightening octave so low that the floor and chairs vibrated with each word. "Just as she killed me when I failed. She won't care why. She has waited too long. Now you carry the curse forever."

The silver plate blasted up off the table, struck the ceiling, and stayed there. The candles snuffed out and the candlesticks spun in place like a quarter of children's tops.

Then from the center of the table rose a ghostly image of the crocodile-headed Sobek. It faced Alice with a head half as large as the table. It continued to rise until it was eye-to-eye with Alice. Its shoulders were so broad that the edges of the table seemed to keep them from fully passing through.

Sobek's eyes glowed a fiery blue. "Enough!" he roared.

The amulet yanked Colin from his chair and dragged him to the wall where an ancient dagger hung on display. He struck the wall hard, chest first, and looked like he was glued there with his arms out at his sides.

"Return to your cage!" Sobek commanded Alice.

Sobek opened his mouth and like a dragon sent a torrent of blue flame and smoke at Alice. It hit her in the chest, swept her off her feet, and slammed her into the wall behind her. The backblast of it rocked Rick and Rose's chairs back. Only Humphrey leaning in on both from behind kept them from falling over.

A pair of translucent, feathered hands shot up from the table behind Sobek. One clamped down on either side of the god's neck. The torrent of blue flame stopped. Sobek looked skyward and cried out with a bellow that shook the artifacts in the room and knocked pictures from the walls. The hands pulled Sobek back down into the table and he disappeared.

The spinning candlesticks abruptly stopped. A wide, jagged crack ripped across the top of the table. The heaviness in the air dissipated.

Alice collapsed to the floor. Colin sighed, pushed himself away from the wall, and wobbled on his feet. The amulet dropped inert to his chest. He'd hit the wall so hard that he'd pressed the old dagger hanging there into the plaster.

Humphrey relaxed his grip on the Sinclairs' chairs. Rick grabbed Rose's hand.

"Are you okay?" he said.

Rose took a deep breath. "Yes. You?"

Rick nodded to Alice. "Shocked but doing better than her."

Alice wasn't moving. Rose slid back her chair and went to her.

"Rick," Humphrey said, "I been to county fairs in three states and ain't never seen nothing like that."

Colin staggered back to the table, massaging his neck. He took off the amulet and shoved it deep in his pocket. “This amulet would have severed my neck if I hadn’t let it drag me. I’m not sure how far it would have pulled me if the wall hadn’t been there, but it felt like it would have been a long way.”

Rose wondered if that would have been such a bad thing. She knelt beside Alice. Her eyes were closed, but thank God the woman was breathing.

Rose laid a hand against her cheek. “Alice, can you hear me?”

Her eyes fluttered open. “Yes. I…how did I get here?”

Rose helped her to her feet. “What’s the last thing you remember?”

“I was sitting at the table and the flames went blue. That had never happened before and it took me by surprise. Then I was here on the floor.” She looked at the broken table top. “Oh, my, what happened to my table?”

Rose helped her back to the table. Rick righted her chair so she could sit down.

“You don’t remember channeling my grandmother?” Colin said.

“Your grandmother?” Rick said.

“I’ve seen plenty of pictures of her,” Colin said. “She was a famous actress. That was exactly who Alice looked like when she spoke in that strange voice.”

Alice felt all over her face with her fingertips. “My dear, I hope I look like myself again.”

Rose patted her shoulder. “Completely.”

“She said this Mut-em-menu had killed her because she failed,” Humphrey said. “What did that mean?”

“In 1914,” Colin said, “she had a trip to Egypt planned with members of the Hermetic Order. Well, the Great War and German U-boats cancelled that plan. She tried to reschedule the trip, but the Great War made that impossible. She died in 1917 before the war ended."

"Died or was killed?" Rose said.

"The newspaper reports in family albums say she died of cancer. My mother would never talk about it. But cousins spoke of madness overtaking her followed by a suicide the family covered up. I never got the true story."

"Maybe you just did," Rick said.

"And it doesn't look like Sobek was very happy about you getting it," Rose said.

"Sobek?" Alice said.

"He appeared and broke the table," Rick said.

Alice blanched. "Oh, my stars. I think we could use some tea to settle our nerves. At least I know I could."

She got up and wandered out of the room.

Rose whirled to face Rick and Humphrey. "That woman and this whole silly secret order have no idea what they're doing."

Colin stepped over. "Now see here, that is a bit harsh."

"A harsh fact," Rose said. "This house has more fake items in it than P.T. Barnum's. And the supernatural event we just experienced took Alice by surprise. I bet the only thing she'd conjured up before this was disappointment from anyone paying for her services."

"Be that as it may," Colin said as he patted his pocket, "she did activate this amulet to show us the way to Sobekneferu's tomb."

"Didn't seem like the guy with the crocodile head was too keen on us talking with Colin's grandma," Humphrey said.

"Alice opened the door for something very dangerous," Rose said.

Rick ran a finger along the crack in the table top. "Looks to me like that door is broken and closed. While it is, I say we find that tomb."

"Are you kidding?" Rose said.

"Rosie, remember we're broke. We need to find that treasure or we'll become permanent dishwashers in some Cairo restaurant."

"I don't have the gas to even get us back to Europe," Humphrey said.

"I agree we go," Colin said.

"People spend lifetimes searching for lost tombs in Egypt and come up with nothing," Rose said.

"We have a divining rod." Colin pulled the amulet from his pocket and laid it in the palm of his hand. It twisted around until it pointed to the place where he'd hit the wall. "The amulet is willing to show us the way."

Alice returned with a tray of cups and a teapot.

Colin intercepted her. "Alice, we're not going to have time for tea. We need to set out to find Sobekneferu. Have you any tools for doing an excavation?"

"Of course! The Hermetic Order set me up with some, but I never had to use them. Lucky for me the local traders had so many artifacts available that I never had to go dig up my own."

Rose sighed at the poor woman's ignorance.

"We're going to borrow those tools," Colin said, "and go out and do a little digging."

CHAPTER ELEVEN

Rick was happy to discover that Alice did have a nice assortment of unused digging tools in a shed behind her house. It included picks, shovels, brooms, and the like. One of the things Colin had promised had actually come to fruition. Given Colin's otherwise perfect record of lying, Rick was certain that was just a coincidence. Everyone selected a few tools to take back to the wagon.

Rose stopped the group before they got out the shed door. "According to Dr. Khalifa, the most likely location for Crocodopolis is south of here around a mostly dried up lake. Was that amulet pointing south?"

Colin thought about it a moment. "Yes, that wall I hit is facing south, so yes."

"Sounds like that's the place to go," Rick said.

"That's got to be seventy-five miles from here," Rose said. "Too far to go by wagon. We'll need to fly and find a place to land in the desert."

"Got a quarter tank of fuel, Miss Rose," Humphrey said. "I can make it there and then back here for gas, but not much more."

"Then I say we go back to that hovel we spent the night in," Rose said, "grab our baggage, and then take that and our tools to the plane. We take off and we don't tell Donkor where we're going."

"Why not?" Rick said.

"Because I don't trust him," Rose said.

"Without him we'd have slept on the streets somewhere," Rick said. "He's local. He might have some tips for us going there."

"She's probably right, Rick," Humphrey said. "Nothing turns honest men dishonest like a sack full of treasure. We oughta keep the destination to ourselves."

"Mum's the word," Colin said.

"Then the votes are in," Rick said. "We keep Donkor in the dark."

The group carried the tools out to the wagon. Donkor sat in the front seat. He smiled at the sight of the tools.

"So, we are going digging, then?" he said.

Rose's distrust of the man had made Rick more wary of the dragoman. His interest in the group's plan didn't help Donkor's case.

"Eventually," Rick said. "First we're going back to the apartment."

Donkor looked disappointed. "As you wish."

With the gear loaded, everyone climbed in and Donkor headed back to the apartment. The wagon seemed to crawl along.

"Think you can hurry that donkey up?" Colin said.

"The day grows hot and the donkey sets his own pace. All the coaxing in the world won't make him a race horse."

By the time they returned to the apartment, Rick guessed it had taken almost twice as long as the morning trip out. Colin told Donkor to wait at the wagon. Everyone else went up to the apartment with Rick in the lead.

When they got to the apartment door, Rick stopped the group and put a finger to his lips. He pointed to the handle.

The door was ajar. Rick was certain he'd closed and locked it.

He waved Humphrey forward. Then he pushed open the door and the two rushed in. Rose was right behind them.

The room was a shambles. Bags had been dumped open and rifled through. Flipped over chairs exposed undersides that had been torn up in search of something. The balcony door was open and the wind billowed the thin drapes.

A boy stepped out of one of the bedrooms. He wore a shorter version of a man's long robe. He was hatless though it didn't seem like one could have contained his mop of curly, black hair. He looked shocked to see anyone else in the room. The group had the door completely blocked.

"Stay right there," Rick said.

The boy bolted for the balcony door.

Rick and Humphrey moved to catch him, and instead bumped shoulders.

That was all the delay the boy needed. He beat them through the doorway, then vaulted over the balcony and into space. Rose gasped.

Rick and Rose dashed out to the balcony. Rick looked over the railing expecting to see the boy sprawled on the ground, dead. Instead, he saw the wide yellow awning of the bakery below. The boy was running down the street, already half a block away.

"The kid had to have used the awning to break his fall," Rick said. "Got to give him credit for quick thinking."

"Or he robs the place every time someone checks in and already had his escape route planned," Rose said.

Colin and Humphrey joined them on the balcony.

"My stuff is a mess," Humphrey said, "but nothing's stolen."

"Same with me," Colin said.

"For once, it pays to be dead broke and destitute," Humphrey said. "You got nothing to steal."

"Or we scared him off before he could," Rick said.

"Or he didn't find what he was looking for," Rose said. "The only thing of value we have we took with us."

"The amulet," Colin said.

"Rosie," Rick said, "how could he know we have it? No one does."

"Um," Colin said. "Donkor knows. I may have mentioned it to him."

"How could you do that?"

"Well, he implied that I was some kind of neophyte, lacking any idea what I was doing. I felt I had to prove him wrong."

"And instead," Rose said, "you told him about the amulet and proved him right."

"If Donkor knows we have it," Humphrey said, "he could have told anyone in Cairo. Funny we got robbed at this apartment he so conveniently found for us."

"And the trip back here was so slow we could have walked it faster," Rose said, "as if he was making sure that kid had time to ransack the place."

Rick scratched his chin. "Those pieces all fit together. Once Humphrey gets us into the air, Donkor will be left behind. If he's planned any sabotage, that will put an end to it. And when we get back down to the cart, no mention of this burglary to Donkor. I want to see his reaction when he's not sure about the cards he thinks we're holding."

Everyone packed their bags and brought them back to the wagon. Donkor appeared dismayed at the sight.

"The lodgings are not satisfactory?"

"No," Rick said. "They were swell. Let's head back to the airstrip."

Donkor grimaced, then covered that with a very forced smile. "As you wish."

The donkey seemed to have a miraculous stamina recovery and set a much faster pace back to the airfield.

Halfway there, Donkor turned to Colin. "I hope you are not having to travel far today. Sandstorms are common this time of year."

"Not far," Colin said. "Our original plan has come to naught, so we're hopping over to join an expedition at work in the Sinai."

True to form, Colin again showed what an awful liar he was. Rick hoped Donkor couldn't tell as well.

When they got to the airfield, Donkor parked beside the plane. Humphrey hopped out, unlocked the cabin door, and began to inspect the plane. The others unloaded bags and equipment and stowed them onboard. As Rose and Colin finished and took their seats onboard, Humphrey completed his walkaround, gave Rick a thumbs up, and entered the plane.

"I would be honored to continue in your service," Donkor offered. "It pays to have a translator and someone familiar with the customs of my people."

Rick clapped him on a shoulder and smiled. "The other expedition has all that covered. You've been a great help."

Rick took the cash from his pocket and peeled off three day's pay for Donkor. He didn't like how little money that left in his hand. Rick passed the cash to Donkor. "Here's an extra day's pay since we're leaving early. You're going to want to move that donkey before the engines start. They get pretty loud."

Donkor took the money without any reaction. He went back to the cart and led the donkey away.

Rick felt a swell of relief. Rose had been right about Donkor. She'd also been right about Colin being untrustworthy. Of course he wasn't going to admit any of that to her. Then again, he wouldn't have to. He was certain she'd be reminding him of it many times. He climbed into the plane and stood between Colin and Rose.

"Is our Crocodopolis compass still working?" Rick said.

Colin pulled the amulet from his pocket and laid it flat in his palm. It spun about ninety degrees and pointed south.

"Seems to be pointing to treasure," Colin said.

"Then let's go get it," Rick said.

CHAPTER TWELVE

As he watched the Tri-motor rise into the sky, Donkor gripped the donkey's reins so tightly that his fingernails gouged his palms.

This plan had gone horribly wrong despite everything he'd done right. After years of surveillance on the Hermetic Order in England, his contact there had alerted him that the amulet of Mut-em-menu had been found. Even better, they would not have to make a plan to steal it and get it out of the country. An idiot named Colin Farr was going to bring it to him.

From the cable Farr had sent to England, Donkor had deduced where and during what window of time the Englander's plane would arrive. His patient waiting had paid off and he had been at the airport when the Tri-motor landed. The three extra Americans with him had been an unwelcome surprise and foiled his plan to rob Colin of the amulet right away. But he had decided to play the role of faithful dragoman, and bide his time.

Fortune rewarded him again. When the fools had no place to stay, he'd pounced on the opportunity to lodge them in his brother's empty apartment, where his nephew Muhammed could steal the amulet. But the foreigners had returned early, or the boy had started late, or both. For whatever reason, the boy had come away empty-handed. Now the foreigners and the amulet were gone, and so was his chance to get his hands on Sobekneferu's treasure. Donkor had no idea where the foreigners were headed.

But he knew who could help him find out.

***

Alice Meriwether looked with dismay at her cracked table. There was no repairing it the way it had split across the grain. Even if she could, all the painted features had been blistered and charred by whatever had happened when she'd blacked out.

A knock sounded at the door. She went and stood behind it. Alice wasn't expecting anyone.

"Who is it?"

"It's Donkor, the Sinclairs' dragoman. There's been an accident."

Alice gasped and threw back the deadbolt.

As soon as she did, the door burst open and sent her staggering backward. Two large men in black fezzes and checked scarves charged in. They grabbed Alice by the arms and pinned her against the wall. Donkor followed and stood face-to-face with her.

"Or should I say there's going to be an accident," he said, "and you'll be the victim if you don't tell me what I need to know."

"Y-you can't treat me like this," Alice said. "I'm a British citizen."

"Then you're one of a long line of colonialist thieves." Donkor gave the artifacts in the room a cursory glance. He picked up a vase, scoffed and returned it to its shelf. "Yet your house is full of nothing worth stealing. A collection of cheap fakes."

Donkor did a double-take when he saw the summoning table. He stood beside it, incredulous. "In a collection of trash, you have a jewel? Where did you get this?"

Alice thrust out her chin. "That piece was entrusted to me by the Hermetic Order of the Golden Dawn prior to my departure. We'd used it to serve tea and they wanted me to have a reminder of home."

Donkor knelt and inspected underneath the table top, then rose and grabbed the table's edge. "You stupid woman, so ignorant of our ways. You don't even know what this is. It is a summoning table, described in the ancient *Book of the Dead.* Perform the correct ritual and it becomes a telephone to the gods."

Donkor ran a finger along the crack. "It will never do that again. But it still sings of residual magic. You did not use the proper ritual. You activated the table in the presence of the supernatural."

"I-I don't remember what happened after the amulet started to glow. Colin—"

"The amulet of Mut-em-menu was here? With that power this would not become a telephone to the gods, but a doorway. No wonder the table broke. You are lucky the house is still standing. Who has the amulet now?"

"Colin had it when they left."

"And where were they going?"

Alice was afraid to tell them anything. She knew these men were killers.

Donkor stepped over and grabbed her by the throat. He squeezed and she choked.

"For the last time, where are they going?"

Alice waved a hand to let him know she surrendered. He relaxed his grip.

"I don't know," she rasped out, then pointed to the dagger on the wall that Colin had crushed into the plaster. "They didn't know, either. The amulet was leading them that way."

Donkor went to the wall. He plucked the dagger from the plaster and produced a shower of white dust. He rolled it across his fingers.

"Another modern fake, but it too has residual magic from contact with the amulet." He laid the dagger in his palm. It made a lazy turn until it pointed south.

"It points south, to old Lake Moeris, legendary home of Crocodopolis."

The dagger rolled out of his hand and dropped. It stuck point first in the floor.

"The residual magic is gone," Donkor said.

"How will we find them?" one of the goons said.

"We'll listen for rumors and look for a plane in the desert. They will not be hard to find. Then we just need to watch until they uncover Crocodopolis and all its treasures."

"I won't say a word to anyone about your plans," Alice said.

Donkor plucked the dagger from the floor and pointed it at Alice.

"No, you certainly won't."

CHAPTER THIRTEEN

Rick's view from the co-pilot's seat at 5,000 feet was all clear, blue sky and endless, yellow sand. They'd flown past some small settlements, and the lands around the Nile had been lush and green, but the southwest turn they had taken now traversed parched, open desert.

Colin stood back between the pilot and co-pilot seats, staring down at the amulet lying in his palm.

"We still on course?" Rick said.

"Absolutely," Colin said. "Wait, a little to the left now."

Humphrey put the plane into a gentle bank. "Say when."

Colin kept laser-focused on the amulet. "There! Level out."

Humphrey brought the plane level. It bounced around a bit. "Lots of thermals out here."

"And not much else," Rick said.

"I say, hold on," Colin said. "I think we passed it."

Colin stuck his hand out into the cockpit. The amulet was pointing behind them.

"All I saw down there was a whole lot of nothing," Humphrey said. "Watch the engine temperatures, Rick."

Humphrey throttled the plane back and circled the area.

"Now it just keeps pointing in different directions," Colin said.

"We must be close," Rick said. "Let's set down somewhere and see what the amulet says then."

"There's a sad little excuse for a road over there," Humphrey said. "I cotton to landing on that more than soft sand."

"You think it's safe?" Colin said.

"I don't see no traffic, do you?"

Minutes later, the Tri-motor bounced twice as it landed on the road. It was indeed a poor excuse, uneven and barely wide enough for the Tri-motor's tires. Humphrey taxied to a flat spot off the road and shutdown.

Colin held out the amulet. It pointed off the nose of the aircraft. "We have a solid direction again."

"We're home, Rosie," Rick called between the seats. "You can pop that cabin door."

The door opened before Rick had finished the sentence.

"I'm way ahead of you," Rose said.

The four of them exited the plane. The air was as hot and dry as that around a blacksmith's hearth. The sun beat down like hammer blows. All four of them went instinctively for the shade under the wing.

"Hotter than the Devil's front porch out here," Humphrey said.

Colin kicked at the hard-packed earth. "Egyptians don't know how to build a road."

"That's no road," Rose said. "Not this far out. That's a camel caravan trail, pounded flat by hooves for centuries. It probably started back at Lake Moeris and continues on to an oasis out there somewhere."

Rick stepped over and gave it a close inspection. "I don't see any tire tracks here but ours, or any footprints."

"Good," Colin said. "Likely we won't be disturbed then."

"Or be able to get help in the event of an emergency," Rose said.

"Then, we'll resolve to not have any emergencies," Rick said with one of his charming smiles.

"All your schemes turn into emergencies," Rose said.

Rick checked his watch. "We have a few hours of daylight left. Might as well follow that amulet and see where it takes us."

"Capital idea." Colin climbed back into the plane and returned with three shovels. "Just in case we find something interesting."

"Hold on," Rose said. "This desert isn't as empty as it looks. That travel research I did included a long list of dangerous creatures that live out there."

"Big desert, little animals," Rick said. "I'll play those odds."

Rick and Humphrey took a shovel each. Colin took an azimuth off the amulet and pointed off the nose of the aircraft.

"Tally ho," he said and began to walk. The rest followed in his footsteps. After a hundred yards, Rose stopped the group.

"Wait," Rose said. "What's that up ahead?"

About two miles away, what looked like a thick, brown rope went from the ground to a thousand feet in the air. It swayed back and forth in waves from the ground up to the end.

"Now that's strange as hell," Colin said.

The undulations quickened. The brown stream widened, far more at the top than the bottom.

"Aw," Humphrey said. "That there's just a dust devil. Seen 'em in Arizona."

"I don't think dust devils get that large," Rose said.

The dust devil headed toward them. The base of it left behind a gouge on the desert floor where it had sucked sand into its maelstrom. And not only was it growing closer, it was growing larger.

"That's no dust devil," Rick said. "That's a tornado."

"Can't get a tornado out of a clear, blue sky," Humphrey said.

"And yet, here one comes."

"See?" Rose said. "Emergency."

Rick looked for somewhere to take shelter. He saw nothing but flat desert. "Everyone back into the plane!"

The four ran back to the Tri-motor. The whooshing sound of tons of sand swirling in the air closed in from behind them. Wind-driven grains began to sting the back of Rick's neck.

The group reached the plane and clambered through the cabin door. Rick was the last one through. Sand blasted into the cabin from behind him. He whirled around, slammed shut the door, and locked it.

Humphrey went to the cockpit. Colin sat in the last seat in the rear. Rick took a seat beside Rose and wrapped his arms around her.

The sandstorm hit. Grains pounding the plane's metal skin sounded like a million wild animals scratching at it from the outside. The air was so thick with sand that it blotted out the sun and the cabin turned to dusk.

Rose buried her head into Rick's shoulder and wrapped an arm around his waist.

The wind picked up and howled like a wounded beast. The plane rocked and then bounced. The wing struts moaned and dust sifted in through the seams in the aircraft's skin.

Rick hoped Rose couldn't hear how fast his heart was pounding.

"Ricky, she can't take much more of this," Humphrey called back from the cockpit.

Suddenly, the sandstorm blew itself out. The plane went still and the remaining suspended sand dropped like rain against the cabin. Daylight returned. Rick released Rose.

"I can skip doing that again," she said.

Colin sat in his seat, eyes closed, head bowed, both hands clasping the amulet that again hung from his neck.

"Colin?" Rick said. "You okay?"

Colin's eyes opened. He squinted as if the light was too much for him. Then he let go of the amulet and sat straight up. "Quite well, thank you."

Humphrey came back into the cabin. "That sand pitted some of the windscreens pretty bad. Better check the rest of the plane."

He opened the door and sand sprinkled from the seals. Humphrey hopped out and hot air rushed in.

Rose wrinkled her nose. "Smell that?"

Rick breathed deeply. "Smells like dirt and…something else."

"It's that same scent of decay that old books or abandoned houses have," Rose said. "The desert didn't smell like that before."

Colin jumped up and went to the door like a man refreshed after an afternoon nap. "All right, back at it then, shall we?"

He jumped out.

Rick turned to Rose. "Well, Colin responds pretty well to brushes with death."

"Here's hoping that's not a quality we're going to need."

CHAPTER FOURTEEN

Colin felt invigorated and ready to discover the queen's tomb.

Back at Alice's house, when he'd come face-to-face with what appeared to be his grandmother's ghost, and then been thrown into a wall by the amulet, he would have tossed in the towel if everyone else had agreed to. Only the desperation of being dead broke in a strange land had kept him from quitting whether anyone else did or not.

But the sandstorm had changed all that.

When the sand had blotted out the sun and the plane seemed like it was about to fly off without the aid of engines or pilots, Colin had cowered in the back of the cabin with his eyes closed. He'd been certain these were his last minutes on Earth.

Then he heard a female voice say "Ask me."

He looked over at Rose. She was weathering the storm tucked into Rick, and that hadn't been her voice anyway.

"Ask me," the voice said, "and I will have Sobek intervene."

He knew there was only one person the voice could be from. He pulled the amulet out from inside his shirt. It had a faint blue glow. Mut-em-menu was reaching out to him, just as she had to his grandmother decades ago.

In desperation, he clasped the amulet between his hands and begged for supernatural assistance from Mut-em-menu.

And it had happened. The storm ceased and they'd all been saved. There was no other way to classify it than as a miracle. Mut-em-menu was going to put her power at his disposal. He expected plenty more miracles to come.

Rose checked her watch and then looked up at the sun. "There isn't a lot of daylight left. Why don't we all clean up the plane and start fresh in the morning?"

"Butter my butt and call me a biscuit," Humphrey said. "Miss Rose has the best plan of all."

"As usual," Rose said.

Colin was ready to head straight for the tomb, daylight or moonlight made no difference. He was certain they would be protected. But he didn't dare tell the others that. Mut-em-menu would stay his secret for now. Sobekneferu's tomb had been there for thousands of years. It would still be there tomorrow.

***

Later that night, Rick and Rose sat alone off the tail of the plane. Rick marveled at the explosion of stars above them. Between a clear, moonless sky and no ground lights from cities or towns, no other lights competed to wash out their beauty.

"That sky's one hell of a sight," he said.

"And except for the positions of the planets," Rose said, "those stars are in the same place Sobekneferu and her priestess saw them tens of thousands of years ago. One of the earliest references to the constellations was from Ptolemy, a Greco-Roman astronomer from Alexandria, Egypt, in the 2nd century, and this was pretty close to the view he had."

"You are a veritable fountain of historical knowledge."

"One of us has to be."

Rick smiled. "If we both were, imagine how dull our conversations would be."

Rose punched him in the arm. "Idiot. There's one bit of history Dr. Khalifa filled me in on that I didn't like. He said that Sobekneferu's burial spot wasn't known because she was killed somewhere out here on the way to Crocodopolis by the people who overthrew her."

"And?"

"Well, do you think they took the time to bury her with treasure for the afterlife? I wouldn't count on it."

"Whatever we find will be worth something," Rick said. "And it must be worth a lot if she set a supernatural trap to defend her with a sandstorm."

"And that sandstorm doesn't worry you about what else her magic might have in store for us?"

"That magic was pretty weak. The storm petered out fast, didn't do any real damage. I think her ju-ju has lost its mojo over time."

"I'm going to pretend that statement was in English. For your information, that curse 'mojo' as you call it stays potent for centuries. You know about the curse of Tutankhamen?"

"That was a movie with Boris Karloff, right?"

Rose rolled her eyes. "No. The real Pharaoh Tutankhamen. His tomb was discovered by Howard Carter about sixteen years ago. There were curses on the tomb promising death to any who disturbed him. Since opening the tomb, at least six people from that party have had mysterious deaths."

"Out of how many people working a famous tomb site that big?"

"I don't know."

"Hundreds?"

"Probably."

Rick wrapped an arm around her shoulder and gave her a squeeze. "Then I like our odds."

Rose pulled away. "We already got hit by a supernatural sandstorm. You don't think a curse could happen?"

"Sure. Just not to us. And sandstorms aren't all supernatural. Besides, with Colin's amulet pointing the way, we'll be in and out before the curse even knows we're there. You worry too much."

"And you worry too little," Rose said.

"Another example of why we're a match made in Heaven."

***

For a place that got unbearably hot during the day, the Sahara Desert turned unbelievably cold at night.

Colin had planned to sleep outside, but had quickly opted to sleep inside the plane with the others, encouraged by the almost immediate chill in the air after sunset. That chill and safety in numbers were all that kept him from heading out to find the tomb by himself.

Mut-em-menu abhorred the delay. Her voice rang loudly, clearly, and persistently in his head. She demanded that he continue on. He could sense her rising anger and impatience after waiting thousands of years, and finally being walking distance from her queen. Her request, no, her *order* to leave was almost irresistible. But he knew the risks of traveling alone at night across the desert were too great, even if Mut-em-menu dismissed them. He stayed put.

Morning confirmed that he'd made the right call to sleep in the plane. When Humphrey opened the cabin door just after dawn, he let in a blast of cold air that made Colin shiver and pull his blanket up over his head.

After a futile forty minutes of trying to stay warm beneath a blanket, the rich aroma of coffee convinced him that warming himself from the inside was a better idea.

He stepped out of the plane to see Humphrey and the Sinclairs standing around a homemade stove that looked like it started life as a hydraulic fluid can. They were drinking coffee and munching some crackers. Colin joined them and Rose handed him a mug and a few crackers.

"Ready to rediscover the missing pharaoh?" Rick said.

Inside Colin's head, Mut-em-menu screamed for him to get moving now.

"Most certainly," he said.

"And is the amulet ready?" Rose said.

Colin definitely knew the answer to that question. He stuck the cracker in his mouth and pulled the amulet out from under his shirt. He held the chain between two fingers and the amulet pointed off the wing of the plane. "It's champing at the bit to help us."

With his toe, Rick nudged a bulging backpack at his feet. "I've packed us food, water, flashlights, and a few tools. But most important…"

Rick reached in and pulled out a big burlap bag. According to its markings it originally held fifty pounds of Idaho potatoes.

"…a sack for treasure," he concluded.

"Ever the optimist," Rose said.

"Optimist? I'm being a pessimist. Guaranteed we'll find so much loot that we'll make King Tut's tomb look like an empty warehouse."

Behind Rick, a stream of sand ran out from an engine cowling and onto Humphrey's shoulder. The pilot's face screwed up in concern. He reached up and popped open the cowling. A bucketful of sand poured out. He danced to one side and avoided the yellow shower by inches.

"Aw, hell," Humphrey said. "This plane might be so full of sand it won't take off. Plus, I'll need to make sure that storm didn't sandblast a hole in any of the fuel lines. Y'all best go on along without me."

"Nah," Rick said. "Like I said before, we stick together on this trip. C'mon along and I'll help you with all that when we get back."

Humphrey rested a hand on Rick's shoulder. "Now I can probably get her shipshape in about six hours. No offense Rick, but with your help, it would probably take twelve."

Rose stifled a laugh. Rick grimaced.

"Look," Rick said, "I don't know how long we'll be leaving you by yourself out here."

"Rose could stay here with him," Colin offered.

Anger flashed in Rose's eyes. "Not on your life.. I'm not some fainting female. And I trust Humphrey to make good decisions by himself more than I do Rick."

"That might be an insult," Rick said, "but I need to think it through."

It took all of Colin's self-restraint to not crow about how they had the mystical power of Mut-em-menu on their side, and they had nothing to worry about. Instead, he said, "Then the three of us should go. The pendant said we were close when we landed and we're quite alone out here. I think it will be smooth sailing."

Before anyone could raise a further objection, Colin swung a shovel up over one shoulder and set out in the direction the amulet had pointed, and as the voice screaming inside his head demanded.

CHAPTER FIFTEEN

Rose didn't see they had any choice but to follow Colin. She and Rick grabbed shovels, picks, and the packs containing flashlights and provisions and set out after him.

As the three crossed the desert sands, the temperature seemed to rise twice as fast as the sun did. Rose had brought a wide-brimmed hat and was glad for it. Rick sported a beat-up pith helmet from their Savannah shop. He'd seen his idol Errol Flynn wear one in the desert adventure *Another Dawn*, and Rose hadn't been able to talk him out of bringing it.

It could have been worse. Rick could have decided to wear the ridiculous bycocket cap the actor had worn in *The Adventures of Robin Hood.*

Colin tromped across the sands hatless and with shirtsleeves rolled up to his biceps. His fair skin was already pink from the sun and Rose was certain that would turn to a deep, painful burn before long. But the man seemed unfazed by that, the heat, or the effort it took to keep a good footing in the sand. Since she'd first met him, Colin had struck her as an effete weakling. The desert air appeared to have strengthened him. Her fears about she and Rick having to carry his weight were alleviated, though she started to wonder if his new-found confidence might make him too reckless.

A mile or so ahead, a strip of escarpment rose from the dunes like the back of a surfacing whale. The darker brown of the stone contrasted with the lighter, yellow sands. Colin was making a beeline for it. At times, he seemed to talk to himself, often in an animated way.

Rose thought that was a bit disconcerting. Plus, despite the long trek so far, he had sped up enough to leave a widening gap between him and Rick.

"Pace yourself, Colin," Rick called out. "We might have a long way to go."

"We don't," Colin said without looking back. "We're quite close. Can't you feel it?"

Rick gave Rose a quizzical look. "Can you feel it?"

"All I feel is sand in my shoes," she said. "I think the sun might have gotten to him."

A half hour later, Colin stood at the base of the escarpment. The craggy rock wall rose at least a hundred feet high in front of them. Weather had eroded fissures in the face and delivered an accumulation of darker sand down along the base.

Rick and Rose caught up to Colin. He stood facing the wall. The amulet dangled at the end of its chain in his left hand. It pointed at a downward forty-five-degree angle to the base of the escarpment.

"This is the spot!" Colin said.

"Inside solid rock?" Rick said.

Colin closed his eyes and winced. "Ahh! Yes! I know!"

He reopened his eyes. "Here. The amulet is showing us. Underground."

Rose swung the shovel off her shoulder and drove the spade into the brown sand before her. She inspected the sand as she slowly sifted it off the shovel's blade.

"That makes sense," she said. "All this dark sand weathered off that rock face. More of it drifted in over time. Thousands of years ago, none of this was here and the wall would have been exposed much further down."

Colin hadn't waited for Rose's agreement. He'd already tossed aside his pick and gripped his shovel with bizarre zeal. He started wildly shoveling sand from the base and sending it flying behind him.

"So, I guess we're digging," Rick said.

He and Rose joined in.

They dug for hours. Rick and Rose took regular breaks for water and rest. Colin would not be deterred from the mission. Rick had to pull the shovel from his hand to make him stop and take a drink. Two gulps later, Colin was back at it.

It took a lot of digging, but eventually they uncovered a rough-cut slab of stone several inches thick and about six feet long on all sides. It lay flat against the now exposed face of the wall. There was no way this was the result of a rock slide. The protective covering of the sand had kept the chisel marks around the edges as sharp as the day they were made. The three of them stood in the hole they'd dug in front of the stone.

The pendant hanging around Colin's neck pointed straight out at the slab.

"She's in there," Colin said.

"Then let's get her out," Rick said.

Rick went to one side of the stone and Colin the other. They each pounded the flat end of a pick into the crack between the slab and the wall. Then they stepped back and gripped the handles to pry the stone away.

"Rick?" Rose said.

"Not now, Rosie."

"But if you—"

"Rosie, give me a minute, will you? Now stand back. Okay, Colin, on three. Ready?"

"Ready," Colin said.

"One…two…*three*!"

The two heaved against the stone. After four useless seconds of struggle, they quit, panting hard.

"Okay," Rick said. "We loosened it up. Let's give it another shot."

"Rick," Rose said. "Before you hurt yourself—"

"I'm not going to hurt myself. We've got this. Right, Colin?"

"Right-o."

"One…two…*three*!"

The two attacked the stone again. Three seconds into it, the handle on Rick's pick snapped off near the head. Rick tumbled back against the side of the pit and raised a cloud of dust.

Rose looked away and stifled a laugh.

"Damn," Rick said. "Now what?"

"Let the rock do the work," Rose said.

"Huh?"

Rose drove her shovel into the sand at the base of the stone. "Dig away the sand in front of the stone. Its own weight will topple it."

Rick stood and dusted himself off. "Now, that's a fine idea, Rosie."

"If you'd let me tell it to you in the beginning, we'd still have two picks."

Rick looked properly chastised. He stepped over and grabbed Rose's shovel. "Colin, what are you waiting for?"

Colin tugged at his pick. It hung wedged between the stones. He gave up and grabbed a shovel.

The two of them began digging around the base of the stone. Rose climbed up to the edge of the pit for a better view and a safer space. After several minutes of digging, the crack between the stone and the wall widened a fraction of an inch at the top.

"It's starting to go," Rose said.

Rick and Colin kept digging, though further from the middle. The two picks stuck at the sides came loose and dropped to the ground. Then the stone made a kind of moaning sound. Rick and Colin jumped away to each side just as the slab toppled forward. The top of it crashed into the edge of the pit and left the stone at an angle sloping down into an exposed cave. The angled sunlight only lit the first few feet of it and left the rest in darkness.

A blast of dark, fetid air blew out of the cave and Rose had to grab her hat to keep it from flying off. The air reeked of things long dead with a trace of sulfur. Though the air was unnaturally hotter than the outside temperature, it still gave Rose a chill as it blew past her.

The blast didn't faze Colin in the least. He jumped up on the slab and then hopped into the cave. Rick moved to follow him.

"Rick!" Rose said. "We have no idea what's in there."

"Whatever it is, it's been dead a long time." Rick pulled two flashlights from his pack. "C'mon."

All Rose could think about was the curse that had befallen the people who had entered the tomb of Tutankhamen. She knew the idea of curses was superstitious nonsense, but there was no denying what she'd read, and there was especially no denying the very creepy feel that opening this cave had given her. Her husband's tendency to leap before he looked wasn't what they needed here.

Rick disappeared into the cave. Rose climbed up onto the slab. When it fell it had sent up a cloud of sand and dust that had settled back on the face of the stone. The sand had partially obscured cartouches carved into the face. While thousands of years old, protection from sunlight and the elements meant that the original brightly-colored paint still adorned them, Rose knelt and swept a few clean with her hand.

She didn't like what she saw.

She hurriedly cleared away more of them with wide sweeps of both hands. Then she jumped to her feet and whirled to face the cave.

"Stop!" Rose shouted. "Both of you!"

Rick and Colin stood about two yards into the cave. Both had turned on their flashlights. They pivoted to look back at Rose.

"Look at these cartouches," she said.

"You can read them?" Colin said.

"No, but I can recognize them. Some of these are the same warning cartouches that were carved into Tutankhamen's tomb."

"All rubbish," Colin said. "Those types of warnings were probably carved on every tomb."

"Maybe on the outside," Rose said. "But on the inside? The people doing the burying didn't want anything to call attention to the burial from the outside, but they still wanted a curse to be invoked on anyone who stumbled across it. This is no warning. This was part of an actual ritual."

"Rosie," Rick said. "I think the sun's gotten to you if you are starting to believe in ancient curses."

Rose took Rick's flashlight and played the beam across the walls. The same sequence of cartouches ran along both sides at chest height, just where the burial team would have chiseled them. Rose thought this was an awful lot of work to do if these people hadn't been true believers.

"Well, we've come too far to stop now," Colin said. The pendant pointed deeper into the cave. "We're almost there. I'm quite sure of it."

Rose shined her flashlight into the cave. The light petered out without touching a rear wall.

"Whoever did this burial went to a lot of effort to deny Sobekneferu an afterlife," Rose said, "and to keep any potential supporters from finding her. Doesn't that tell you something?"

"It tells me there are artifacts in this cave no one has seen for thousands of years." Rick's eyes flashed and he smiled. "Priceless artifacts."

Colin headed deeper into the cave. Rick pulled a third flashlight from his pack and followed him. Rose had no choice but to go with them.

Sand coated the cave floor, likely tracked in by the builders, blown in through the tiny gaps at the covering stone, and sprinkled down from the ceiling. While Colin and Rick had their lights illuminating the wall and the depths of the passage, Rose had hers focused on the ground ahead.

"Everyone stop," she said.

Colin and Rick froze. Rose's beam lit up a perfectly straight gap in the sand just ahead of where Rick stood. It was about four feet long and narrower than a pencil. If someone had been using an oil lamp like the builders had used at that time, it likely would have gone unnoticed.

"How come there's no sand right there?" she said.

Colin knelt and brushed some sand across the gap. It disappeared down the fissure. Rick joined him and they swept away a flat panel of red stone about two feet wide. Another panel sat on either side of it. Rick rested a hand on the center panel as he cleared away the one on the left.

The panel made a cracking noise.

Rose grabbed Rick's shirt and pulled him back. As she did, a crack ran across the panel and spawned others. Then the panel shattered. The pieces dropped away into darkness, followed by an echoing crash. The missing panel left a gap over a yard long.

The three pointed their flashlights down into the gap. There was a pit over a dozen feet deep below with very rough edges and a jagged floor.

"That panel wasn't stone," Rose said, "just clay made to look like stone. Something to defend against graverobbers."

"I'd like to point out," Rick said, "that they wouldn't need that if the curse really worked."

Colin pointed his flashlight across the gap. It lit up a shadowy box a few yards away. Without a word, Colin backed up, and then with a running start, leapt across the chasm. He landed on the other side and made a skidding stop in the sand.

"That reckless idiot," Rose said. "There could have been another trap on the other side."

"But there wasn't," Rick said. "And whatever the builders left over there still is. Can you make that jump?"

Rose wasn't sure, but she certainly wasn't going to admit it since Colin had made the leap. "Of course I can."

Rick made a sweeping gesture across the gap with one hand. "Ladies first."

Rose backed up, took a deep breath, and dashed for the gap. She jumped and was certain she wasn't going to make it. But just as she was about to scream, her feet hit the other side. She took two more steps to regain her balance. A split second later, Rick landed beside her with a smile.

"See, piece of cake. You worry too much, Rosie."

"And you worry too little."

"Let's see what treasure we've just discovered."

They moved ahead to where Colin stood over what appeared to be a stone casket. Unlike a royal sarcophagus, this one didn't have the carvings on the lid depicting the idealized image of the mummy within. This one contained a painted scene of Egyptian priests watching a battle between gods. Horus and Anubis flanked Sobek. Each had a golden spear thrust into the crocodile-headed god's sides. Sobek was screaming in pain. At his feet lay an unconscious woman in a pharaonic headdress.

The amulet hadn't lied. It looked like they'd found the burial place of the heretic pharaoh.

CHAPTER SIXTEEN

Tears welled in Colin's eyes as he ran a finger over the painting on the lid of the sarcophagus.

"It looks like they left a record of the queen's last moments on her sarcophagus," Rose said.

"Talk about adding insult to injury," Rick said.

"So, the army didn't kill her on the way to Crocodopolis," Colin said. "She'd made it to Sobek's temple. But somehow, they stormed the complex and defeated her and Sobek."

"It looks like they called on a couple of other gods to give them a hand," Rick said.

"Not just some," Rose said. "The one on the left with the head of a falcon is Horus, preeminent god of Egypt, and the jackal-headed one is Anubis, master of the Underworld. That's a combination too powerful to overcome."

"But then why move Sobekneferu here?" Rick said. "Just let the sandstorm bury her along with Crocodopolis."

"One last indignity," Colin lamented. "A permanent separation from all she had accomplished."

"Or maybe she was still alive, and part of her punishment was to watch her monumental city destroyed."

"And they interred her in a special sarcophagus they brought with them specifically for her," Rose said. "The way trappers bring a specific cage out on a hunt."

Standing this close to the sarcophagus gave Rose an even stronger case of the creeps. She played the beam of her flashlight along the walls and empty floor of the cave.

"Rick, there aren't any artifacts here we can take home. We certainly can't move that sarcophagus. Let's get out of here, report this place to the antiquities authority, and cut our losses."

"What about inside the box here?" Rick said. "Mut-em-menu's pendant says the matching pendant is inside, right Colin?"

Colin held the pendant out over the sarcophagus. It pointed straight down, pulling the chain taut as a harp string. "Guaranteed."

"They wouldn't bury her with something that valuable to take into the afterlife," Rose said.

"We won't know if we don't check," Rick said. "We can't fold our hand before we draw our last card."

"Rick," Rose said, "opening this seems like a hell of a bad idea."

Colin ignored the debate. He shoved the flat end of his pick under the lid, held his breath, and leaned back. Stone scraped against stone. The lid rose a fraction of an inch. He exhaled and let it back down.

"Come along," he said to Rick. "Lend a hand now."

Rose was about to warn Rick not to, but he had the excited look he always got when he thought one of his longshot bets was about to come in. He put the tip of his shovel against the seam between the lid and the box.

"Hit it," Rick said to Colin.

Colin leaned back again. This time when the pick raised the lid, Rick wedged the shovel into the gap. The two of them strained against the wooden handles. The lid angled up, then slid off the box. Rick and Colin tumbled backward. The lid struck the ground, flipped upside down, and cracked into multiple pieces. Rose moaned at the loss of the painting on its top.

The three of them crowded around the open sarcophagus and trained their flashlight beams inside. There was no inner sarcophagus. Sobekneferu's body wasn't even bound in linen wrappings. The corpse lay on its back, arms cocked at its sides palms up. The desert air had dried out the body and the mouth seemed opened in a perpetual, silent scream. The simple tunic on the body had decayed to a gauzy remnant.

No pendant hung from the corpse's neck.

Rick lit the hands with his flashlight. The fingernails were all cracked and mangled. Then he shined the light on the inside of the broken lid. Tiny gouges marred the surface.

"Dear God," Colin said. "The bastards sealed her in there alive."

Rose looked closer at Sobekneferu's skin. Even though it was mummified, it looked very strange, almost scaly. That was going to bear some closer scrutiny.

"Rose was right," Rick said. "They didn't bury her with the pendant."

"Yes, they did," Colin said.

He held his pendant out just over the body. The sapphire glowed blue. From within the corpse's torso came a corresponding faint glow.

"She swallowed it before she was captured," Colin mumbled, "to keep it out of the soldiers' hands and ensure that we could be reunited."

The glow in the mummy intensified. Then a pendant matching Colin's exploded out of the mummy's chest. It struck the pendant around Colin's neck. A blinding flare of blue light blasted from the figure eight of joined jewels. A pressure wave followed the light and blew Rose back off her feet. She lost consciousness before she hit the ground.

***

The blast threw Colin back against the cave wall. He smacked his head on the stone. A trickle of warm blood ran down the back of his neck.

And something very alien stirred inside him.

Unlike his grandmother, he'd never channeled spirits or communed with the dead. But since the séance disaster in Cairo, he felt like he'd been doing a little of both. He'd felt something odd, like an internal itch he couldn't scratch, as soon as the pendant began pointing the way to Sobekneferu. The closer they got to the tomb, the stronger the pull from the pendant became.

Then during the sandstorm, he heard the voice for the first time. She hadn't needed to identify herself as Mut-em-menu. Who else could she be?

From the moment he'd taken up her offer for help, it was like he'd opened the door she'd been knocking on since the séance. She'd charged through and tried to take control of him, tried to shut him out of his own body. It felt like attempting to stand up in the face of a mental hurricane.

He'd talked to many mediums during his investigations of his grandmother's history. They'd warned that contacting the dead could be overwhelming. If the spirit has unfinished business with the living world, it will try to force itself back into it. Then, instead of the medium passing along its messages like a telephone receiver, the spirit will take over the whole phone booth. Proper mediums mentally trained themselves to defend against such an attack.

Colin had no training. He hadn't even planned on contacting the dead himself. But somehow, he'd held his own against the Egyptian priestess. Perhaps some innate ability his grandmother had possessed had been passed down to him. Or perhaps he was just mentally stronger than he'd given himself credit for. Mut-em-menu's voice had grown stronger, her demands more insistent the closer he'd gotten to the tomb, but he'd held his own against her.

Until the pendant erupted from Sobekneferu's chest.

The flash and the wave of energy that knocked him down were external. But something stronger happened internally. He experienced a flood of emotions that were not his own: anger, relief, vengeance. The spirit freed from the tomb had hit him full force.

Then he felt joy, and in stereo.

That spirit of Mut-em-menu that had been dogging him was overjoyed by the presence of Sobekneferu. And Sobekneferu greeted Mut-em-menu with the emotions built up over thousands of years of separation. The priestess told the queen how she'd promised to never abandon her. The queen replied how the priestess had always been her most loyal servant, and how now together they could right the injustice done to Sobek.

Then the two spirits turned on Colin.

This time, he could not put up a fight. He was overwhelmed, beaten down, and diminished. All his mental energy drained away like water from un unplugged basin. Only when there was almost nothing left did the two women break off their mental assault. To his own surprise, he'd survived.

But he'd survived because they'd allowed him to. Like a pair of cats with a terrified mouse, they were not ready for the kill. Instead, they'd push and pull behind his façade of free will. He was well aware that when the time was right, they would take over. His helplessness horrified him.

This was the disaster the spiritualist mediums had warned him about.

CHAPTER SEVENTEEN

Back at the aircraft, Humphrey was wondering if he'd ever get all the sand out of it. Every cowling he'd opened had revealed a space choked with yellow grit. The storm couldn't have done more damage if Humphrey had left funnels wedged into every gap in the plane's skin.

A long hose and some compressed air would have been a big help, but instead all Humphrey had was a two-inch-wide paint brush from the tool kit. With that, he swept out most of the sand and cleaned off any fuel lines and control cables. The last thing he needed was to have the sand chafe a hole in any of those. That still left plenty he couldn't get to. He hoped that once he started taxiing, seventy-five miles an hour of rushing air blasting through the gaps in the metal skin would clear out the rest. It had better. Every extra pound of weight on board used fuel he couldn't spare.

If Rick and Rose didn't find some things worth selling, Humphrey was going to be up a creek without a paddle. He'd spent damn near everything he had to get the plane ready and fueled to get them out here. If his friends came back to the plane emptyhanded, there was no way they'd get the fuel to make it home. Then once the Egyptians discovered his stranded, foreign plane, he was certain they'd impound it, and then the show was really over. He'd likely end up imprisoned for illegal entry, aviation violations, and just being an American. Given his checkered smuggling past, being a World War veteran wasn't going to be enough to get the U.S. Embassy to help him out of a jam like that.

Humphrey closed the cowling on the Number Three Engine and went back to the tail. He lay down on the hot sand and shimmied underneath the fuselage. There was a compartment here he used to hide illicit goods from inspectors. It was about six feet long and three feet wide, but only two feet deep at the most. Tucked between the fuselage skin and the floor of the cabin, this panel was the only access. Humphrey had cleverly routed the tail control cables around the space but it looked like they ran through it. In hundreds of customs inspections, the hiding spot hadn't been discovered.

Humphrey pulled a screwdriver from his coveralls and set the blade against one of the rivets in the panel. But it wasn't a rivet, it was a rivet-looking cover over one of two quick-release latches like on the engine cowlings. He popped the cover off, then did the same for the other hidden latch holding the hinged panel in.

He was pretty sure this compartment would be empty. He'd made certain it was well-sealed. No point in having the cargo inside ruined flying through a rainstorm. But Humphrey figured it didn't hurt to check. And besides, with any luck at all, Rick and Rose would return with plenty of things to hide inside.

Humphrey popped the first release free. Sand trickled out of the widened panel gap and onto his chest.

This compartment sure ain't sealed as well as I recollect, he thought.

The other latch flexed and then popped open. The panel dropped. What felt like fifty pounds of sand dumped onto Humphrey's face and chest. He hoped his reflexes had shut his eyes fast enough.

They hadn't shut his mouth, and now it tasted like a day at the beach in there. Grit felt like it was sanding his teeth. He choked and sputtered as he shimmied back out from under the plane. Once he thought he was clear, he rolled over and pulled a rag from his pocket. As he coughed and spit sand from his mouth, he wiped the sand from his closed eyes. He blinked them open and offered up thanks that they didn't feel gritty.

His mouth was a different story. He stumbled over to his canteen he'd left under the shade of the wing. It took three swishes to get most of the grit out of his mouth. The sand that filled his collar sprinkled down inside his coveralls. He had a bad feeling he was going to be standing naked in the desert while he tried to shake the sand out of his underwear.

Overhead, a vulture screeched. Startled, Humphrey spun around and banged his head on the engine cowling. He cursed and stepped out from under the wing. A bird's shadow flashed by at his feet.

He looked up to see a brown and white vulture circling the plane about twenty feet off the ground. The bird flew much faster than any vulture he'd ever seen, and made impressively sharp banks at each turn. It seemed to keep one eye trained on Humphrey as it circled.

Vultures always gave Humphrey the willies, with their bald red heads and creepy eyes. Feasting on the rotting dead didn't help any, either. But they were not hunters and easily scared away from their carrion.

He got the distinct impression that this vulture might uncharacteristically attack.

But on its third trip around the plane, it broke off its inspection and flew straight down the old camel caravan trail. Miles down that trail, Humphrey thought he spied a cloud of dust. He didn't like the look of that.

He dashed around and into the plane, returning with his binoculars. He trained them down the trail and focused. Three men in white robes and covered faces were coming his way on motorcycles. At least one of them looked like he had a cartridge belt around his waist and a rifle slung across his back.

Humphrey didn't need to waste time seeing if the others were armed as well. One was more than enough. It seemed the vulture had done him a favor by warning him of these bandits' approach.

The question was, what did he do now? Humphrey's pulse raced. Three-to-one were odds even Rick would turn his nose up at.

He felt like a pad of butter just dropped on a hot skillet. He couldn't start running. There was nowhere to hide with nothing but flat desert for miles. But he also couldn't stay. He didn't speak Egyptian, so reasoning with these three wasn't going to be an option, as if bandits responded to that anyway.

Why did I let Rick talk me into this mess?

CHAPTER EIGHTEEN

Rose's head spun as she lay on the cave floor. The blue flash had left a sea of dots swirling across her field of view. She fought back a wave of nausea.

Rick crawled over beside her. "Rosie, are you okay?"

Her vision cleared and she sat up. "Just woozy."

"I can't say I saw that coming," Rick said.

They both grasped the end of the sarcophagus and pulled themselves to their feet. Inside the box, the desiccated remains of the former queen had turned into a human-shaped pile of gray dust. Rose wasn't going to get that second chance to inspect her skin.

Colin's hands appeared and gripped the other side of the box. He pulled himself upright. He didn't look as disoriented by the blast as Rose felt. In fact, he looked calm and more self-assured than Rose had ever seen him.

"Colin?" Rick said. "How are you?"

"Perfect." Colin's voice had no inflection.

Both pendants now hung fused together on the chain around his neck. A pinprick of blue light sparkled in each.

Rose pointed at the pendants. "The pendants are fused?"

"Reunited," Colin said, "as they were destined to be even after thousands of years apart."

He looked down into the sarcophagus.

"The blast disintegrated Sobekneferu," Rose said.

Colin scooped up a handful of the ashes and then let them sift back down into the box. "This is no more the queen than the chaff is the wheat."

Rose thought that was strange. No one pawed through human remains without emotion and Colin hadn't uttered anything so philosophical in all the time they'd been together. She gave Rick a questioning look.

He nodded and went to Colin's side. He touched Colin's shoulder. "How about we get out of here into some fresh air?"

The points of light in the pendants went dark. Colin looked up from the ashes in the box and blinked several times. The blank look on his face reverted to a more natural look of slight confusion. "Yes, capital idea. Fresh air."

The three of them retreated back to the cave opening and stepped onto the toppled sealing slab. Even though the air was furnace-level hot and Rose had to shade her eyes from the blazing sun, it felt like paradise compared to the oppressive tomb.

"Oh, yes," Colin said. "This feels much better. I think that experience took more out of me than I imagined."

Rose worried that it had done the opposite, and actually put something into him.

"We found the pharaoh's burial place," Rick said. "But this was a bust. There's no treasure, no artifacts."

"Even the painted lid is broken and worthless," Rose said. "As if we could have gotten it out of here anyway."

"There is the pendant," Rick said. "Those sapphires can bring a good price."

Colin wrapped his hand around the fused pendant. "No, this pendant is priceless. And it is now an even stronger guide. See?"

He released the jewels. They floated up and pointed off to his left.

"They point the way to Crocodopolis," Colin said.

"Are you sure?" Rick said.

"Yes, quite. Just as I was sure the pendant was directing us to this tomb. Even more so, in fact."

"We've been gone most of the day already," Rose said. "We should head back to the plane and go tomorrow."

"We are already halfway there," Colin said. "Going back to the plane means a full day's hike tomorrow in the sun."

"I'm with Colin," Rick said. "If we're going to come away from this trip with anything valuable, we need to find Crocodopolis."

"The pharaoh was entombed in this empty space on purpose," Colin said, "to deny her succor in the afterlife. But Crocodopolis was buried in an instant by a sandstorm. Every bit of treasure and tribute will still be untouched within it. The longer we are out here, the more likely we'll attract the kind of local attention we don't want."

"We still have plenty of water," Rick said. "I say we go for it, Rosie."

Rose knew risk-taking Rick would want to go straight for the treasure. She remained unconvinced.

"If the city was swallowed up in a sandstorm," Rose said, "how will we find it and get into it?"

"We found this place and got in," Rick said. "We'll find Crocodopolis the same way."

"You mean by blind luck?"

"My luck isn't blind. It's legendary."

Rose rolled her eyes.

"I'm pushing on," Colin said. "You two can backtrack our footprints to the plane if you wish."

Rose was ready to do just that. But once back at the plane, with Colin having the pendant, there'd be nothing to point her the way to Crocodopolis. Plus, once the treasure was uncovered, Rose didn't trust Colin alone with Rick. She guessed Colin had either figured all that out, or honestly didn't care if they accompanied him.

"All right," she said. "Let's follow the pendant's course."

***

A few hours later, they hadn't seemed to have gotten anywhere. The desert dunes ahead of them looked no different from the ones they'd crossed. Rick was starting to wonder if perhaps his luck had run out on this trip.

Colin blazed the trail a few yards ahead of him, guided by the pendant. He hadn't spoken a word since they'd set out, staying silently focused on following the pointing jewel around his neck.

Rose walked beside Rick, matching his pace. One of the things Rick loved about his wife was her ability to pull her own weight, and usually quite a bit more.

"Holding up okay?" he asked as they slogged through the sand.

"Just peachy."

"Colin is made of stronger stuff than I'd thought."

"If that's still Colin. Doesn't he seem different since that blast in the tomb?"

Rick didn't want to admit it. "He's a little more focused."

"Focused? He's obsessed. I thought he was a little too intense about finding Sobekneferu. But he was completely disinterested compared to how he wants to find Crocodopolis."

"Well, so do we if we want to pay our way home."

"Not like he does," Rose said. "And did you catch the times he's referred to events in the past as if they'd happened to him?"

"Well, yes. That was a little strange. Maybe he's having a bit of a breakdown with all this stress and his mother's recent death."

"We need to keep an eye on him." Rose looked up at the sun as it dipped into the western sky. "We need to find this place soon. We don't want to be caught out here at night."

"We haven't seen a soul since we got here. Even if we had something to steal, I don't think we need to worry about getting robbed."

"It's not people I'm worried about," Rose said. "It's the wildlife."

"We haven't seen a single creature," Rick said.

"Because they aren't stupid enough to be walking around during the hottest part of the day like we're doing. They all hunt at night. Another thing you'd know if you'd read the Egypt book I gave you."

"As long as one of us knows, that really should be enough."

They crested a dune and headed down the other side in a half-walk-half-slide. The ground leveled out and dunes surrounded them. Colin kept marching forward.

Ahead of them, a hissing sound broke the silence. The three froze. Rick shielded his eyes from the sun and searched the ground.

"There!" he said.

He pointed to a snake half-buried in the sand about ten feet in front of them. Its tan scales were a near-perfect match for the sand. Only the black diamonds along its back gave it away. It raised its head and flicked its tongue. What looked like a horn sprouted over each eye.

"I wonder if that's venomous," Rick said.

"A Saharan horned viper," Colin said. "Very poisonous."

"Again," Rose said to Rick, "something you'd know if you'd read the Egypt book."

"What do you say we give this boy a wide berth?" Rick began a leftward sidestep without taking his eyes off the snake.

Then a hiss arose from his left. He whirled to see a second snake slithering from that side.

"This is getting uncomfortable," Rick said.

Suddenly, like a chorus of punctured tires, hissing sounded from all sides. Six snakes now formed a ring around them.

Rick swung his shovel off his shoulder and faced off against the nearest snake. Rose did the same. Colin grabbed his pick with both hands and raised it over his shoulder.

The snakes began a slow slither toward the group. Each moved slightly side to side, closer and then further apart. Rick couldn't decide which snake would strike first and which to aim for.

"Rick, we won't be able to get them all," Rose said. "When we hit one, another will strike. They're going to be too fast."

Rick moved back-to-back with Rose.

Colin stood his ground and gave his pick a wild swing in the direction of one of the snakes. "You think you can stop me? I'll kill every one of you!"

Rick admired Colin's spirit, but Rose was right. He wasn't betting on them getting out of this alive.

From the dune above came the laughing bray of a hyena. The unnerving sound sent a shiver down Rick's spine. The last thing they needed now was another predator in the mix.

More hyenas answered that first call from the surrounding dunes. Then about a half dozen popped up around them. Against the blue sky the yellow dogs with the black spots stood out. They were larger than the average pet dog, with much more muscular front legs, and as Rick saw it, much larger and sharper teeth.

"Word gets around fast," Rick said. "Scavengers are already waiting to pick at our bones."

The snakes closed to just feet from the three.

The hyenas cried out, then charged down the dunes, cutting ragged trails in the sand. The snakes paused and swiveled their heads to face the threat. Before the snakes could strike, the hyenas pounced on them. Four of the dogs hit their targets paws-first. They clamped their teeth on the snakes, and then raised their heads with the writhing serpents in their jaws. With a chomp and a crunch, the snakes went limp.

Two dogs dove for their prey and missed. But those snakes knew the tide of this battle had turned. They began a rapid, slithering retreat up the dunes.

The foiled hyenas would not be deterred. They followed and pounced. In no time, each hyena had a dead serpent dangling from its jaws. Then the pack charged up a dune, crested the top, and disappeared.

Rick exhaled and could not believe their luck. Rose sighed and leaned against her shovel. Colin rested the head of his pick against the ground.

"That was unreal," Rose said.

"The group of us attracted the snakes," Colin said, "and then the snakes attracted the hyenas. And lucky for us those hyenas were hungry."

"That's what you think just happened?" Rose said. "Those hyenas arrived to rescue us."

"Dear Rose," Colin said, "the creatures may look like dogs but they certainly don't act like them. Hyenas and humans are not compatible."

"I know. I read about the wild animals out here." Rose shot Rick a withering look. "Unlike other people. And nothing about what just happened was normal. Neither the snakes nor the hyenas are ever out in the middle of the day like this. Snakes also don't hunt in groups. Above all, the two species don't engage in pitched battles like that, especially just feet away from human beings."

"Except that they just did," Rick said. "And when your longshot finishes in first place, you don't question how the jockey did it, you just collect your winnings and smile."

"In your research," Colin said to Rose, "you did see that hyenas eat snakes, didn't you?"

"Yes, they do, among a lot of other things."

"Then being out here in this wasteland, it seems pretty normal that they'd take this meal of opportunity, even if it meant dodging some humans to get it."

Rose didn't look like she was ready to accept that explanation. "Rick, we're stepping into a fight much bigger than we can handle. Look, getting attacked by a nest of snakes isn't normal, right?"

"I guess not."

"And wild hyenas saving us like Rin Tin Tin is pretty bizarre, right?"

"Agreed."

"Both of those events need some kind of supernatural spark to light them up, and the source for each wasn't the same. I think there's some grudge match between the gods going on here, with one of them wanting us to find the city, the other desperate that we don't."

"Rose," Colin said, "you're reading a bit much into this."

Rick thought the whole conversation silly. As long as they were all alive and snake-free, what difference did it make?

"If this wasteland is going to turn into some battlefield for the gods," Rose said, "we'd be crazy to take one more step forward."

"That won't be necessary." Colin took the joined pendants from his neck and held them by the chain out in front of him. The jewels hung straight down.

"We've already arrived," he said.

CHAPTER NINETEEN

Out on the ancient caravan trail, Donkor spotted his vulture flying in from the west. He skidded his motorcycle to a stop. His two henchmen pulled up on either side of him.

A falconer's glove sheathed Donkor's left hand and extended halfway up his bicep. Bands of ancient Egyptian cartouches ringed the portion above his wrist. A symbol of Nekhbet, the vulture-headed goddess, was emblazoned at the top. While the glove looked to be made of leather, only Donkor knew it was made of tanned human skin. Such were the sacrifices demanded by Nekhbet for her assistance.

Donkor raised his glove over his head. The vulture screeched, tucked its wings, and then dove nearly straight down. At the last second it spread its wings eight feet wide. The bird flared, and landed on Donkor's forearm. The creature weighed almost twenty pounds, and Donkor leaned back to balance the weight.

Both of the henchmen rolled their motorcycles away from the bird and gave it fearful looks.

The vulture looked at Donkor, then raised its bald, purple and red head in what he swore was a look of superiority. Strapped to its chest with thongs around its neck and below its wings was a golden likeness of Nekhbet, the conduit for which the god, or at least its power, flowed into the bird.

The bird hopped sideways, then pecked at a series of cartouches.

Donkor smiled as he mentally translated the message. "Nekhbet has delivered the foreigners to us. Their plane is on the ground ahead. Remember not to kill the one with the amulet. With it he will lead us to Sobekneferu."

The vulture took off and flew west.

The world of the gods of Egypt was a tumultuous one. Eternal life and extraordinary power combined to create a web of jealous intrigue. Always one god was pitted against another, fueled by its unshakable belief that it should rule over all others and over mankind. So it had been when Sobek rose to challenge Horus, and then Horus and Anubis had struck him down.

When Donkor had sought the favor of the gods to discover Sobekneferu's tomb, and then Crocodopolis, Nekhbet, the goddess of vultures, had answered his call.

During Sobek's rise to power thousands of years ago, the vulture goddess had surreptitiously supported him. But like her vultures, she was a creature of opportunity, and in the end had betrayed Sobek to Horus and Anubis, avoiding their wrath.

Donkor had hoped this universally shunned god would be keen to put herself back at center stage. He had offered her prayer and sacrifice, and she had responded. It was a toss-up whether she agreed to avenge Sobekneferu's death, or to do penance for it. All that Donkor knew for sure was that Nekhbet had pledged her power to help him.

And she had happily provided him with this vulture pet. The creature terrified him at first. His henchmen were still repulsed by its chilling appearance and its reputation for feasting on the dead, but most of all by the tangible sensation of evil that oozed from the bird. Donkor had learned to embrace all those attributes. The goddess had given him the instructions on how to channel her assistance through this vulture.

The vulture spread its wings and took flight. The three men revved their motorcycles and followed the bird.

It wasn't long before Donkor spied the Sinclairs' plane parked on a flat spot just off the caravan trail. He motioned for his henchmen to spread out and approach the plane from different angles. One broke right and the other left. Moments later, they had the plane surrounded from about thirty yards away. The three stopped, straddling their idling motorcycles. The two henchmen unslung the rifles from their backs and pointed them at the plane.

Donkor looked the plane over closely. He didn't see any movement, but several engine cowlings hung open, and the glass in the windscreen facing him had been shattered. Perhaps the plane had been forced to land.

The vulture circled overhead, then landed on the tip of the center engine's propeller. It let loose a piercing screech. If there had been anyone in the plane, he was going to step out to investigate that.

No one did.

Donkor motioned the henchmen to approach the plane. They laid their rifles across the handlebars and motored in. Donkor met them at the side of the aircraft. The three killed their engines.

The plane was dead quiet. The cabin door was locked from the outside.

"Search around the plane for any clues about where the Sinclairs went," Donkor said.

The two henchmen nodded and dismounted. One began to circle the plane. The other rolled his motorcycle up beside the fuselage. He climbed up on the seat and looked into a cabin window.

"No one and nothing much in here," he called back over his shoulder.

Donkor went to the open engine cowling. He found a note wedged up inside and pulled it out. It read:

Rick,

Saw bandits coming and had to take the tent and high-tail it out of here. Got food and water for two days. Meet you back here then.

Humphrey

Donkor searched the sands around the plane. There were no footprints, likely erased by the desert wind. He wouldn't be able to track which way Humphrey went.

But the note told him something important. The other three had set out to find Sobekneferu, which meant they had been able to use the pendant for directions. Finding the pilot wasn't important. Finding the other three was what he needed to do.

The henchman on the motorcycle went to hop off. Instead, the bike toppled over in the soft sand and sent the man sprawling across the ground with a shout. Donkor shook his head in disgust. Everyone he hired seemed to end up being an idiot.

The second henchman returned. "There's nothing here and no footprints."

"We don't need footprints." Donkor stepped away from the plane and locked eyes with the vulture. He raised the gloved hand over his head and made a circular motion. The vulture alighted and flew high in a flash.

The first henchman dusted himself off and walked over to Donkor and the other.

"The foreigners are looking for Sobekneferu," Donkor said. "The vulture will find them."

"What if they have already discovered the tomb?"

"If they have, and aren't headed back here, that means they've also discovered the location of Crocodopolis and are heading there. Either way, we are the winner. Until we find Crocodopolis, the Englander needs to be kept alive. You can kill the others."

The vulture returned and let out two short screeches. It made a circle above Donkor, then flew south.

"The bird has found them," Donkor said. "Let's go."

The second henchman went to his motorcycle and started it up. Donkor did the same. The first henchman righted his motorcycle and tried to start it. The kick-starter locked up. He tried it again to no avail.

"Something's broke."

Donkor seethed. "Ride tandem with him. Let's go!"

The first henchman strapped his rifle across his back and took up an uncomfortable position on the second henchman's bike.

Donkor gunned his engine and followed the vulture. This close to returning the reign of Sobek to Egypt, he wasn't about to let the stupidity of one of these men get in his way.

***

As soon as the sound of the motorcycles grew faint, Humphrey let go of the hatch to the Tri-motor's hidden compartment. It opened and he tumbled out and into the sand. Sweat plastered his clothes to the skin. He was certain that if the men had lingered any longer, he would have either passed out or his sweaty hand would have lost its grip on the cover. Either would have opened the door and exposed him to Donkor and his men.

And he was sure one of the men on the bikes was Donkor. Even though he was speaking in Arabic, Humphrey recognized the voice. After all, who else would be out here looking for the four of them anyhow?

This definitely confirmed Rose's suspicions that Donkor had been working against them the whole time. But now the situation was much worse, because the men with Donkor were armed and "Sinclairs" was the one word out of Donkor's mouth that Humphrey understood.

That meant they were hunting his friends. Rick and Rose had no idea how much danger they were in, and Humphrey guessed wherever they were would be just as desolate as right here, and that was no place to confront armed thugs.

Humphrey rolled out from under the plane. A motorcycle lay on its side near the wing. He remembered that only two engines had started before the men left. This motorcycle must have crapped out on them. A pair of tire tracks ran south from the plane.

He wondered how they'd know where Rick, Rose, and Colin were. Then he remembered hearing the vulture screech again while he was hiding in the plane. The devious bird hadn't warned him about the approaching men. It had found him for the approaching men, then guided them back to the plane.

"Nobody likes a vulture that's a stool pigeon," he said to himself.

He had to get to Rick and Rose and either warn them about Donkor and his men or help them fight them off. He sure wasn't going to fly to meet them.

But there was a motorcycle lying here.

He dashed over to it and lifted it upright. He and Rick had spent enough time rebuilding Rick's motorcycle that he had a good familiarity with them. He brushed some sand off a few places and checked the basics. Wiring and fuel lines looked good. Carb smelled like gas. The tank wasn't empty. The oil wasn't burned. The thing got here so it couldn't be too far gone.

He straddled it and went to kick start it. The pedal didn't move. He tried again with all his weight into it. The pedal didn't budge.

He ran through several potential causes in his head. Almost none of them were terminal. Almost.

"Hell," Humphrey said. "Reckon if I can fix Rick's motorbike, I can fix this one."

He hoped he was right. If he couldn't get this machine to run, there'd be no help for Rick and Rose.

CHAPTER TWENTY

Rose had trouble believing Colin's assertion that they'd arrived at Crocodopolis. She wanted it to be true and have their trek across the desert finished. But nothing looked special about this place between the dunes.

"Colin, are you sure?" she said.

"Absolutely," Colin said. "The pendant hasn't lied to us yet."

"The legend says that the gods swallowed the place up in a sandstorm," Rick said. "If so, there's no way to know where we'll have to dig to find an entrance."

"Or how deep we'll have to dig with two shovels and a pick," Rose said.

"We don't have to dig at all," Colin said. "Yes, the power of the gods buried Crocodopolis in a sandstorm. But that was thousands of years ago. What one storm buries another one unearths. We're at the heart of the complex right now. These aren't sand dunes around us. These are sand drifts, burying the peaks of temple buildings while the wind partly scoured clear the central plaza."

Rose gave the dunes a closer inspection. They did have a uniformity in placement and spacing that Nature never provided.

"Even if you're right," Rose said, "there still must be twenty feet of sand between us and the original plaza."

"We don't need to dig to the plaza." Colin consulted the position of the lowering sun, then looked to the drift to the sun's left. "This is south. The primary temple faced south, toward the source of the Nile and the source of Sobek's power."

Rose thought that description was a bit too detailed given how little Professor Khalifa had said was known about Crocodopolis. She gave Rick a questioning look. He looked pretty leery as well.

"You suddenly know a lot about Crocodopolis," Rick said.

"I learned a lot from reading my grandmother's research. We just didn't need the knowledge until now." He sized up the southern dune. "For example…"

Pick in hand, he scaled the dune, stopping about two-thirds of the way up. He started scraping away sand until he uncovered a sloped section of polished, white limestone.

"What do you know?" Rick said. "There *is* a pyramid under all that sand. And it's got a nicer finish than the big ones near Cairo."

"They all used to have limestone sheathing like that on them," Rose said. "Over the centuries it was pulled off and reused in other projects."

"Some people have no respect for the dead."

"Well, are you going to pitch in or just lay about down there?" Colin said.

Rick and Rose scaled the dune and took up spots on either side of Colin. Soon the three had about a twenty-foot-long section of the limestone uncovered.

"There, just as I knew it would be," Colin said.

He stood up, faced the pyramid, and reared back with his pick raised over his shoulder, the point aimed for the limestone.

Rose knew there was no way the pick was going to do more than chip this sun-hardened stone. Colin's hands were going to be hurting.

Colin took a mighty swing. Rose winced over the pain the man was about to experience.

The pick crashed through the limestone. More specifically, it crashed through a wooden cover expertly painted to look like limestone. Colin pulled the pick out and then used it to clear away the broken remains around the edge. He revealed an opening about four feet high and two feet wide.

"What is that?" Rick said.

"An escape passage in the event of an attack," Colin said, "as well as a way in if enemies have captured the temple. Sobekneferu knew rivals were all around her and planned for it. This was a fairly common feature in buildings of the period."

Colin stepped into the pyramid.

Rose turned to Rick and grasped his arm. "Okay, I did a lot of reading about building pyramids and temples in Ancient Egypt. There was no mention of anything like what Colin opened up."

"Maybe his Order of the Golden Dawn people know more than the eggheads in museums," Rick said. "Who knows what the spirits they contacted told them. And you can't poo-poo talking to spirits after what we saw at the séance in Cairo."

Rose paused. "Okay, maybe you have a point there. But one other thing. You have to admit that there has definitely been something trying to keep us away from Crocodopolis. First the sandstorm and then the snake attack."

"You're back to that whole mummy's curse thing again?"

"If you accept that it takes something supernatural to bury an entire city in an instant, then you can't dismiss that that same power would keep working to keep Crocodopolis hidden."

"By that reasoning, I could just as easily say that in both instances, a supernatural force has been protecting us both times since we're still alive."

"Exactly!" Rose said. "Like I said before, we're walking into some kind of conflict between gods that's been going on for thousands of years. We need to stay out of there and go back to the plane."

"Rosie, listen to yourself. You've let a few spooky events make your imagination run wild. In the real world, we just found a temple that has been buried for thousands of years. Sobekneferu's treasures are in there, waiting for us to take them home. They might be waiting just three feet inside that entrance. We can't turn around now."

Rose weighed that reality. Going back to the plane emptyhanded left them no way to get home. Yet, getting themselves killed inside a lost pyramid meant they weren't going home either. However, Rick had a knack for making bad decisions sound relatively good, and this was no exception.

"We find something valuable, and then we get out," Rose said.

"I bet Colin will go along with that," Rick said.

"If he doesn't, well, that's on him and we'll send help to get him home when we get back to Cairo."

"Agreed." Rick made a sweeping gesture toward the opening in the pyramid. "Ladies first."

"Oh, no. We go together."

Rick tipped back his pith helmet and puffed out his chest. "Step back, Egyptian gods! Here comes the Sinclairs."

Rick dropped his rucksack beside the opening. He and Rose pulled their flashlights out. Rose stepped toward the temple opening.

"Wait one." Rick extracted the big burlap sack and tucked it into his belt. "We wouldn't want to walk out of there emptyhanded."

They stepped through the opening together. Colin had not waited for them, and given his determination to get here, Rose hadn't expected him to. They stepped out onto a small platform inside the opening. Thousands of years had baked the air dry and stale. On the right side, a set of steps led down into the pyramid. From somewhere down below came the flicker of Colin's flashlight.

Rick and Rose rested their shovels on their shoulders, turned their flashlights on, and began to descend the steps. The staircase was unnervingly narrow, steep, and lacked any kind of railing. Rose took each careful step down with one shoulder leaning against the wall.

They descended several stories worth of steps, deep enough to pass beneath the sand dune's base outside, and then deeper still. Soon the staircase ended at a large room that had to be the original bottom of the pyramid. A wide corridor to the right ended at a pile of sand. Colin stood before it.

"This was the entrance," he said, "the gateway for those coming to worship Sobek."

Rose played her flashlight beam along the corridor walls. Huge, colorful paintings of Sobek subjugating other gods towered over her.

"Looks like visitors were reminded who was the boss as soon as they stepped in," Rick said.

"They came in the hundreds every day to worship the Nile god," Colin said, "and pay homage to the female pharaoh who gave him his rightful place in Egypt."

Rose thought Colin's description a little too vivid and wistful. "You sound pretty sure of that."

Colin startled. "Well, I mean, at least that's what the stories say."

"Check this out," Rick said from behind them.

Rose turned around and gasped. Rick stood with his flashlight illuminating a statue of Sobek that faced the sand-filled corridor. The sculpture was at least twenty-five feet tall, carved and polished from a rich, black rock. One foot was in front of the other and both arms outstretched. The crocodile head looked down at the corridor entrance and its mouth exposed a set of fearsome white teeth.

"If this god didn't scare you before you got here," Rick said, "that statue sure would."

"That expression on the statue is very different from the impassive faces on most statues of the gods," Rose said.

"Sobek is not an impassive god," Colin said.

Rick walked past the Sobek statue. "Hey, there's another passageway behind this statue."

Rose and Colin joined Rick. A corridor stretched out about twenty feet to another set of descending steps.

"Look at this." Colin pointed to a rack of metal oil lamps on the wall beside him. A row of sealed ceramic amphorae lined the base of the wall beneath them. "These were offered to guide visitors coming to worship Sobek."

Rick blew the gritty dust off one. "They've been waiting a long time."

"They shouldn't still be here," Rose said. "The Egyptians buried the city and its worshippers in a cataclysmic sandstorm. The people trapped in here would have used all these lamps and the oil beneath them after they'd been buried. In fact, this whole room should have been filled with sand as the people inside tried to dig themselves out at the main entrance, or used the escape exit now that I think of it. But it doesn't look like anyone did."

"If the lamps were all buried in here," Rick said, "then let's hope the treasure was as well."

"Seriously, this doesn't strike you as strange?"

"Rosie, I don't look a gift temple in the mouth."

Something moved on the floor between them and the steps. Rose lit it up with her flashlight. A green and yellow scorpion about three inches long crawled toward them.

"A scorpion," Rose said. "Just what we needed."

Rick bent to give it a closer look. "It has little tiny claws. I think we're safe."

Rose pulled Rick back upright. "When scorpions have small claws it's because they have toxic venom in that bulb in the tail. That's a deathstalker scorpion. Its venom can kill."

"Unless we kill it first." Colin marched over to it. The scorpion turned to face him with upturned claws.

Colin raised a foot and then crushed the insect with his boot heel. The scorpion made a crunching sound. Colin raised his boot to reveal a gooey mess that clung to his sole.

"Problem solved," he said.

Scratching noises came from the steps. Rose trained her flashlight at them.

The beam lit up a line of scorpions marching across the floor in their direction.

CHAPTER TWENTY-ONE

Rose's heart skipped a beat. All three of them jumped back several feet with shovels and a pick raised in defense.

"We can do this," Rick said. "Just bash and scrape them. They crush easily enough."

"One sting is all it takes to kill," Rose said.

But the line of scorpions coming from below was just a row of scouts. An army of scorpions followed a yard behind them. The deadly insects blanketed the floor from wall to wall. Snapping claws created a chorus of clicks as the insects advanced.

"You see this, right, Rick?" Rose said.

"Okay," Rick said, "but they're still just bugs. How many of them can there be?"

Then more scorpions entered the passageway along the walls and ceiling. All four surfaces were now covered with a twitching, advancing mass of deadly insects.

"This is our cue to get out of here," Rose said.

"No," Rick said, "not when we're this close. This swarm will keep us from ever returning."

"Those things will kill us all," Colin said as he took another few steps back.

Rick turned to Rose. "Head for the staircase to the surface."

"What are you going to do?"

"One of my usual heroic-save-the-day things."

"Those rarely work."

"That's why you're heading for the staircase." Rick gave her a shove. "Go!"

Before she could object, Colin grabbed her by the arm and rushed her back to the steps. Rose got the distinct impression that he was masking his cowardice by seeming to save her. A few steps up the stairway, Rose wrenched herself free and looked over at Rick.

He'd reached down and grabbed one of the millennia-old amphorae of oil. He cracked the top and sloshed the contents across the advancing scorpions on the floor. The insects didn't react. The surge forward continued.

Rick next splashed the walls and ceiling the best he could. The soaking wasn't as thorough as the floor had gotten. Then he threw the amphora up and into the corridor. It landed in the middle of the scorpions with a crash and shattered. Oil splattered across the insects and dripped from their stingers.

One of the scout scorpions reached Rick's boot. He was too preoccupied to notice.

"Rick!" Rose cried out. "Your foot!"

Rick looked down and was startled. He stepped back, then used his left foot to scrape a scorpion off the toe of his right. He pulled a box of matches from his pocket, lit one, and tossed it into the insect mass.

The match went out.

He grimaced and struck another. This time he took a leap into the scorpion mass. He landed on one foot and splattered a half-dozen insects. The survivors scampered away and left a clear ring around his boot. Then they turned and started a rush back toward Rick.

Rick lowered the match until it was an inch from the ground. As the scorpions came within inches of him, he dropped the match.

The scorpion nearest the burning match caught fire. Then in a flash, flames spread in all directions. The insects' advance stopped. Scorpions flailed and jumped as they ignited. Flames raced up both walls, across the ceiling, and met in the middle. Burning scorpions dropped from the walls and ceiling like shooting stars.

Rick dashed back up the corridor, crushing scorpions with each step. He stopped and turned around when he reached clear floor.

The fire reached the puddle where the amphora had broken. A boom sounded along with a flash of yellow light. A ball of flame flecked with burning scorpions billowed from the corridor. The impact knocked Rick onto his back. His pith helmet skipped across the floor. He lay still.

The flame ball dissipated.

But Rick had spilled some lamp oil on his leg. Below his knee, his pants burned like a log in a fire. Rick didn't react.

Rose didn't think twice. She leapt down from the stairway.

She dashed across the room, dodging dead and dying scorpions as she did. She got to Rick's side, dropped to her knees, and pulled off her hat. She beat his leg with her hat until she'd extinguished the flames. Then she cast the hat aside and grabbed his charred pants leg. It was still hot to the touch. Rose tore the pants leg apart to keep the hot fabric from burning Rick even worse. By some miracle, his leg wasn't a red, blistered mess.

Rick sat up, woozy. He blinked twice at Rose as he focused his eyes. "Rosie. Did I get them?"

Rose picked up a burned scorpion by a claw and held it in front of Rick's face. "You sure did."

He managed a weak smile. "Swell. Hey, my face feels warm. Do I look okay?"

His red cheeks and forehead looked like the equivalent of a serious sunburn. The heat had singed his eyebrows and mustache into patchy, curly messes.

Rose rationalized that it would be days before he would see himself in a mirror. "You're ready for your close-up, Mr. Flynn."

"That's a relief."

Rose helped him to his feet as Colin made a tentative return across dead and dying scorpion bodies.

"That was close," Colin said.

"Now will you two admit that something supernatural is defending this place?" Rose said.

Colin kicked at a charred scorpion. "They're just scorpions."

"No, they're *hundreds* of scorpions."

"That spend the day underground, out of the heat. They'd discovered a perfect place to thrive in, coming and going through burrows at gaps in the stones. Our arrival simply brought them out to defend it."

"Like kicking an anthill?" Rick said.

"Exactly," Colin said.

"Is it going to take the arrival of an actual Egyptian deity to convince you?" Rose said.

"If one shows up," Rick said, "I'll be first in line to admit you were right."

Colin shined his light down the corridor. None of the scorpion corpses moved. "All clear. Let's have at it, then."

Colin began a tip-toed walk through the scorpions. Rose grabbed Rick's collar and pulled his ear close to hers.

"Once we find something we can sell worth enough to get home," she said, "we head for the exit. Promise?"

"Just like we agreed," Rick said.

Rose let him go. He picked his pith helmet up off the floor. The front half of it was singed.

"Wow," he said. "Lucky for me this protected my face."

The three of them headed down the steps at the corridor's end. This staircase only had ten steps. At the bottom, the wall behind the staircase contained a huge bronze plate with gear-like teeth on both sides. A wheel attached to a bronze screw on one side of the gears.

Rick went over to the plate. "It looks like this mechanism lowers that plate. Maybe there's some kind of treasury on the other side."

Colin shined his light at the base of the door. Dull, smoke-colored tiles coated a recessed area there that connected to a sluice that ran off into the darkness.

"No, that barrier controlled the water that used to run inside this temple," Colin said. "When the plate was lowered, Nile River water entered, and ran down this sluice into the temple proper."

"Herodotus' description of this place said it had multiple rooms and pools, all containing crocodiles," Rose said.

"Let's see if he was telling the truth," Rick said.

Before them ran a corridor wider than the one above the steps. The sluiceway ran down the center and branched out into rooms on either side. The three traveled down the corridor and entered a room on the right.

Inside was a sunken pool lined in white tile. It was about two feet deep and twenty feet wide on either side. The bottom contained a mosaic of a crocodile. The pool also contained something else. Rose trained her light on it.

It was a crocodile, or what was left of one. It had been massive, about seven feet long. The dry air had mummified the corpse and it looked intact, including the large teeth protruding from its jaws. Rose figured the inside was hollow now, but the leathery hide still held its shape after all these years.

"This is just as Herodotus had described it," Rose said.

"The buried city was cut off from water," Rick said, "and when what was here dried up, the pet crocodiles died."

"Not pets," Colin corrected. "Objects of worship."

They went back to the main corridor. As they continued down it, there were many rooms on either side. Most had pools, some with dead crocodiles in them and some without. A few of the rooms were completely empty. So far, there had been no artifact of value they could take back to the surface.

A few thousand feet down the corridor, it ended at a pair of large, wooden doors. The slate-colored sluiceway ran underneath them.

"If there's anything worth taking back," Rick said, "it's going to be on the other side of that door."

He grabbed the handle and turned it.

CHAPTER TWENTY-TWO

The three entered the final chamber. This one was much larger than the others, over a hundred feet long and about thirty feet wide. The sluice ended at a pool that took up most of the floor.

A sconce on the wall by the doorway contained a lamp. Colin picked it up and shook it. Oil sloshed inside.

"If that oil in the corridor was still good, maybe this is as well." Colin struck a match and lit the lamp.

The lamp cast enough light to reveal that sconces ringed the wall. Colin made a circuit of the room lighting them. When he'd finished, the room was aglow.

The empty pool looked like it had been tiled in gold and glittered in the flickering light. A narrow walkway coming in from each side met at a small platform that rose from the pool's center. Inlaid at the pool's bottom was a relief of Sobek. Near it was another mummified crocodile, this one easily twenty feet long. No doubt it had been the special "pharaoh crocodile" Rose had read about, the one kept in special reverence above all the others.

A spear leaned against the wall on either side of the platform, the only two items in the room.

"I'm noting a distinct lack of treasure," Rick said.

"Except for the walls," Rose said.

The walls contained large, beautiful reliefs painted in vibrant colors. These showed scenes of Sobek slaying armies, bringing rain, towering over fields of crops. Based on the promises of these pictures, the reign of Sobek would be the best thing that ever happened to Egypt. Rose knew Sobek's reign would really have been nothing but bloodshed and turmoil, and was glad it had never happened.

"We can't very well take the walls home with us," Rick said.

Arches between the murals opened to recessed areas like the side chapels in medieval churches. Rick and Rose walked over to the first one and shined their lights inside. Rick gasped and grabbed Rose's arm.

Inside hung rows of shields, large enough to protect a man. They had wooden frames and stretched leather covers. Flaking paintings of Sobek adorned the shields' faces.

"This had to be an armory," Rose said. "Ready to equip the army that would rise to support Sobek."

Rick picked up the nearest shield. The entire piece crumbled in his hands and disintegrated.

"Damn it."

He touched the one behind it. His finger went right through the leather.

"Mummified," Rose said. "Dried out just like the crocodiles by centuries of desert air."

"And now totally worthless," Rick said.

"When this place was full of water, everything would have stored much better."

They moved down to the next arch. Behind it had been racks of bows and arrows. Time had reduced most of them to ash-like piles on the floor. Metal and flint arrowheads protruded from the heaps.

"I'm getting a bad feeling about this," Rick said.

Outside this arch, one of the spears leaned against the wall.

"Funny that that hasn't decayed," Rose said.

Rick gripped the shaft. "It's some kind of metal."

He tugged at it. It didn't move. He strained and tried again to no avail.

"It must be some kind of decoration," Rick said. "It's cemented into the wall and floor. Something else we can't use to buy our way home."

The third arch held something different. The others had unfinished walls, but this one's were painted. The rear wall contained a picture of a female pharaoh and a priestess in battle garb riding in a wide chariot. The chariot sported bright colors and the mounted heads of three crocodiles along the front. Both women wore scale armor breastplates adorned with jewels. Sobek towered over them in the background.

In the center of the room stood the chariot from the picture.

"It looks like Sobekneferu and Mut-em-menu planned on leading the armies of Egypt together under the protection of Sobek," Rose said.

Rick gave the chariot a close visual inspection, comparing it to the picture. "This is the same chariot, detail for detail. Waiting forever for the two riders who will never come."

"If you touch it, it will probably crumble just like everything else."

"I won't even breathe on it." Rick stepped around to the rear. "Jackpot, Rosie. Come look here."

Rose went to the rear of the chariot. On its floor lay the two scale armor breastplates the women were wearing in the picture. Even with a good coat of dust on them, the large jewels were unmistakable.

"Now that's a find," Rose said. "I don't know what's holding that scale armor together, if anything at this point. We're going to have to be very careful retrieving those."

"Colin!" Rick called out. "You have to see what we found in here."

Colin didn't answer.

"Colin?"

Still nothing.

Rick and Rose stepped out of the chariot room. Colin stood on the pedestal in the center of the empty pool. The fused pendants hung on his chest and glowed brightly enough to light up his neck and chin.

“Colin,” Rose said, “what are you doing up there?”

“I-I don’t know,” he said through gritted teeth. “They’re making me stand here. They keep screaming.”

Colin raised his hands to cover his ears. Tears rolled down his cheeks.

“Who’s screaming?” Rick said.

“The pharaoh and her priestess. They say it is time for their return.”

CHAPTER TWENTY-THREE

Above in the Egyptian desert, Nekhbet's vulture circled in a bright blue sky. Donkor and his two henchmen gunned their motorcycles and roared up a dune beneath the bird. They stopped at the crest. To the left, three sets of footprints ran down another dune to a depression below.

Then Donkor spotted what the vulture had been leading them to. On the dune across from him an excavated section revealed a sloped, polished limestone wall with an opening in it. The vulture dove down and perched upon it.

"Crocodopolis," he said. "We've found it."

"So have the outsiders," one of the henchmen said.

"Let's make sure they don't live to tell about it," Donkor said.

The three rode their motorcycles down the dune, across the depression, and up the other side. They stopped near the opening and killed the engines. Donkor dismounted. The vulture took off, made one pass around Donkor, and then headed east, as if saying, "I got you here, the rest is up to you."

The other two men dismounted and went to Donkor.

"This is the Temple of Sobek," Donkor said. "Buried by the wrath of Horus and Anubis and supposed to be his eternal tomb. Inside awaits the riches of Sobekneferu."

One of the two looked worried.

"Ya kabīr," he said, "we were supposed to rob the Westerners. Now we're entering a cursed tomb. I can feel it."

Donkor grabbed the man by the shirt. "Ahmed, all you're feeling is cowardice."

Donkor turned to the other man. "How about you, Fares? Have you also become a little girl frightened by the dark?"

Fares shrugged. "No, ya kabīr. I'm here for the riches."

Donkor released Ahmed. "The Westerners are already inside. We need to find them and, more importantly, find the priceless pendant of Mut-em-menu. That amulet will lead us to the lost treasure."

Donkor retrieved flashlights from the saddlebag on his motorcycle and gave one to each henchman. He slung a coil of rope over one shoulder in case they needed to repel down into the temple. The henchmen chambered rounds into their rifles. Then Donkor led them through the doorway.

They rushed down the stairway, but all three stopped dead in their tracks in the shadow of the towering statue of Sobek. Donkor now had no doubts they were in the right place. He looked upon the statue with awe. Ahmed's eyes went wide and he trembled.

Donkor led the others around the statue to a corridor behind it. Spread before them was a carpet of hundreds of dead scorpions. Some appeared to have been crushed but most had been burned. The chamber still stank of burned oil.

Ahmed recoiled at the sight. "Scorpions! The whole of the desert cannot have this many."

"See," Donkor said, "the Westerners have been here and triggered these scorpion defenders. They'll clear us a path all the way to the treasure."

Donkor dropped the unneeded coil of rope behind the statue. He led them through the corridor and down the steps at the end. He'd been researching Crocodopolis for years and immediately recognized the central sluiceway that fed water to the complex. The channels this supplied would lead him to the treasury as surely as Mut-em-menu's pendant would.

Donkor noticed the water gate behind the stairway. He wondered if shifts in the course of the Nile had left it dry, or, if like what remained of Lake Moeris, it was still fed by an underground spring. He stepped over and placed a hand against the metal plate.

It felt cool.

He called his henchmen over to the large wheel on one side that looked like it would lower the gate and let the water return to Crocodopolis.

"Fares, you and I are heading in after the Westerners. Ahmed, you need to get that gate open right now. The water's final destination is the royal treasury in the Hall of Sobek. It will lead us to Sobekneferu's riches."

***

Back in the heart of Sobek's temple, Rose looked with horror at Colin. He stood over on the platform in the dry pool, hunched over with his hands clamped over his ears. Tears streamed down his scarlet face that was wracked with pain. He screamed. Whatever he was going through looked like it was going to kill him.

Suddenly, Colin's screams stopped. He stood erect and lowered his arms down to an odd forty-five-degree angle to his sides. Normal color returned to his face and now it betrayed no emotion.

Treasure or no treasure, Rose knew it was time for the three of them to get the hell out of here and back to the surface and sunlight.

"Rick, Colin's lost his mind."

Rick stared at Colin, incredulous. "Or something else has taken control of it."

"Let's get him out of here and back to the surface, try to break whatever spell this is."

"Colin?" Rick called out.

Colin didn't respond. He kept staring straight ahead. The fused pendants began pulsing a blue glow against his chest. His eyes were open but there wasn't any consciousness within them.

The sound of running water came from outside the room. Then sandy water trickled down the sluiceway from the corridor. As the water washed over the tiles, they changed color from matte gray to bright blue.

"Where did that water come from?" Rick said.

"I don't know but I doubt the Nile just shifted its course since we arrived."

Rick and Rose went to the corridor. Not only was there water in the central sluiceway, but it was also diverting into all the formerly flooded rooms in the complex.

"Rick, this is bringing the temple complex another step closer to how it was under Sobekneferu," Rose said. "There's no way that can be a good thing."

They returned to the main room. The rate of flow down the sluice increased. Water splattered from the sluiceway into the pool and the tile's dark color shifted to a brilliant blue. The pool began to fill. The mummified crocodile was soon submerged.

"Colin, we need to go," Rick said.

Colin didn't react. Rick stepped over and mounted the walkway to the center platform.

A low, bellowing noise echoed from the corridor. Rick whipped around to check the doorway. "Now what the hell—"

The sound repeated several overlapping times.

Rose's jaw dropped. "I know what makes a sound like that at home."

From the pool below Rick came a splash and a deep roar.

The mummified crocodile was mummified no more. It was as if the water had both rehydrated and resurrected it. The massive beast had become even longer and wider. It swam over to one of the posts in the pool that supported the walkway and slammed it with the side of its body. The walkway swayed. Rick teetered near the walkways' edge.

"Rick!" Rose cried out as she ran to him.

Rick stumbled backward and managed to land beside the pool. Rose caught him before he fell.

The crocodile made a rapid circuit of the pool. The wall around it seemed high enough to keep it from getting out, unless the water that was now rushing in overfilled the pool. Then the situation would get gruesome quickly.

"You know," Rick said, "this might be where we fold, cash in our chips, and walk away from this game."

"There you are!" a voice called from the entrance.

Rose spun around. Donkor and another man brandishing a rifle sprinted into the room.

CHAPTER TWENTY-FOUR

Rick turned around just in time for the henchman to drive his rifle butt into Rick's gut. Rick doubled over and went to his knees.

Donkor drew a pistol and aimed it at Rose. "Standing still would be a very healthy thing to do."

Rose raised her hands. "You know we aren't armed."

"I don't like to take chances."

Rick looked up at Donkor. "We knew you were a snake right from the start."

The henchman raised the rifle butt to hit Rick again.

"No, Fares," Donkor said. "Not until after they've seen the treasures they have led us to, unless she makes a move. Then you can blow his head off."

Fares smiled and placed his rifle's barrel against the side of Rick's head.

"There's no royal treasure in here," Rose said. "The Egyptian army probably looted the place before burying it. Everything they left behind has decayed to dust."

Donkor holstered his pistol and looked around the room in consternation. "No, that can't be. You just haven't discovered it yet. The amulet of Mut-em-menu will show me the way."

Rick pointed to Colin on the platform in some kind of standing coma. "It's all yours. Go take it."

Donkor looked at Colin's bizarre expression and stance. He hesitated.

"The twin amulets are joined back together," he said.

"Reunited at Sobekneferu's tomb," Rose said.

"And those reunited spirits are using Colin like a puppet," Rick said.

"I've come too far to be stopped now," Donkor said. "Foreigners have stolen our riches for so long. Government toadies have imprisoned them in museums here. I am descended from the pharaohs. Sobekneferu's treasures are rightly mine."

"You can drop the 'descended from pharaohs' schtick," Rick said. "Every dragoman in the bazaar uses it."

"But in my case, it is true," Donkor said. "My bloodline traces back to Amenemhat III's brother. The blood that flowed through Sobekneferu's veins flows through mine. For generations we have searched for the amulet of Mut-em-menu, the divining rod that would point to Sobekneferu's treasure. But British grave robbers stole it and it disappeared. That is until this fool Colin started running his mouth to anyone who would listen that he possessed it."

"I knew if he told us about it, he'd told others," Rose said.

"He told anyone he thought could help pay his way here," Donkor said. "There was no point in going to South America to take it from him. He was planning on bringing it back to Egypt. I could wait for him to deliver it to me. And he has."

"It looks like you're too late," Rick said. "The pharaoh and the priestess won't let you take the pendant."

"You think Sobekneferu would not favor her own bloodline?"

Donkor stepped to the end of the catwalk. The pendant rose from Colin's chest and pointed at Donkor.

"You see," Donkor said. "It calls to the rightful heir."

Donkor stepped onto the catwalk. The crocodile in the pool stopped thrashing in the water. Donkor marched forward. The amulet turned and pointed right at him.

Donkor grabbed the amulet and tore it from Colin's neck.

Colin sagged on his feet, as if the power of the women in the amulet had been holding him up. He looked at Donkor and blinked in confusion.

Then Donkor shoved him into the pool.

With an explosion of white water, the crocodile attacked Colin. Waves crested the sides of the pool and drenched the floor. Blood quickly stained the frothing water. When it again went still, Colin's body was gone.

Donkor looked over at Rose. "You two are next into the pool."

CHAPTER TWENTY-FIVE

Rick seethed over Colin's murder. He couldn't wait for the chance to toss Donkor and Fares into the pool for some poetic justice.

Moment by moment since he and Rose had entered the buried temple, their situation had gotten progressively worse. Of course, not as worse as it had gotten for Colin. No matter what happened to himself, Rick was going to make sure that that kind of worse didn't happen to Rose.

He looked over at Rose. She had her eyes locked on him and a very worried look on her face.

Rick gave his head a small shake and mouthed *Don't worry. I have a plan.*

Rose nodded that she understood.

Rick really didn't have a plan, except to fake it until he figured one out.

Donkor stood facing Rick on the platform above the pool. The fused amulets glowed blue in the palm of his hand. Excitement filled his eyes and the teeth in his maniacal grin took on the amulets' blue shade.

Donkor's smile faded. His eyes went wide. The color drained from his face.

"Fares?" he croaked.

Donkor's body shook. He bent over hard at the waist, then backwards to an angle no human spine could have managed. When he snapped back erect, his face had the same blank expression Colin's had when he'd been possessed. Sobekneferu had indeed favored her own bloodline.

Donkor raised the fused pendants above his head, then tilted his head back and opened his mouth. Then he dropped the amulets down his throat and swallowed them.

A blue glow encapsulated Donkor's body. He went completely rigid, still staring at the ceiling. He spread his arms out to either side. A ghostly image began to form above him.

It came into focus, two images superimposed upon each other. They brightened and faded in opposite cycles. The first woman wore the trappings of an Egyptian pharaoh, including the distinctive headdress and holding the crook and flail. The second woman wore the simpler white robe of an Egyptian priestess. One thing they both shared were very similar, malicious smiles.

Apparently, this was more than Fares had expected to happen. He stared transfixed at the two ghostly apparitions. The rifle barrel meandered away from Rick's head.

Rick saw his chance. He grabbed the barrel of the gun, pointed it away from his head, and jumped to his feet.

The startled henchman pulled the trigger. The rifle fired and the bullet blasted one of the floor tiles. The hot barrel threatened to burn Rick's hands.

Rick rotated right. The henchman clung to the rifle to keep from losing it. That was what Rick had counted on. Fares crossed before Rick and lost his balance.

Rick drove the rifle butt into the man's chest, then pushed him backward toward the pool. The man's sandals slipped on the water splashed onto the floor. Rick kept thrusting Fares back. The henchman hit the wall around the pool and tumbled backward. He toppled into the water and went under. Rick released the rifle to keep from being pulled in with him.

Fares broke the surface and stood up in the chest-deep pool, spitting water and looking panicked. He began a splashing, uncoordinated wade to the pool's nearest side.

The crocodile came at him like a torpedo. It broke the surface behind him with wide open jaws. Its lower jaw passed between his legs. Fares screamed. The crocodile snapped closed his jaws and sent Fares face first into the water. As the beast pulled him under, it thrashed left and right for the kill. Its massive body swept the support for the left walkway away and it collapsed into the roiling pool of water.

The water stilled. The crocodile lay on the catwalk wreckage. Fares' body was gone.

Rick tugged at Rose's arm. "Rosie, let's go!"

Rick and Rose ran for the entrance.

"No!" commanded stereo women's voices from the platform.

When the Sinclairs were inches from the exit, a crocodile crawled from one of the rooms beyond to block the corridor. Rick stopped and grabbed Rose to keep her from running out into it. It faced them and bellowed.

They weren't getting out of here.

"You've come as thieves into my city," Sobekneferu said.

"The punishment is death," Mut-em-menu said.

"I don't know how two ghosts are going to kill us," Rick whispered to Rose.

"Death by Sobek," Sobekneferu answered.

In the pool, the crocodile rose and stood on its hind legs.

"The required two human sacrifices are made. The enchanted amulets are here. When our spell from the *Book of the Dead* is complete, Sobek will be freed from his prison and reborn in this crocodile vessel."

The two women began an Egyptian chant in unison.

"Damn," Rick said. "My pushing Fares into the pool played into their hands."

"Fares would have fed one of us to the crocodile if you hadn't," Rose said.

The women's chant grew louder. The water in the pool began to boil up a light mist. The lower legs of the crocodile went pale and then transformed into the legs of a man.

"I don't see a way out of this one, Rosie."

"Neither do…wait." She nodded to one of the spears. "Remember the painting on the sarcophagus? It had a picture of two gods spearing Sobek with spears that looked like those."

"Did I miss the part where we assumed the powers of gods?"

"The picture was allegorical," Rose said, "saying the spears were powered by the gods."

"Well, there must be something special about them. They're the only things in here that haven't turned to dust. But they're sealed to the wall."

"Perhaps only until they're needed."

"An 'In case of Sobek resurrection, break glass' kind of thing?" Rick said. "Even if you're right, I don't know how we'll get to them before the crocodile can get to us. It looks like it's big enough to get out of that pool, even before it transforms into Sobek."

"I know how I can get those two distracted."

"Using what?"

"My woman's intuition," Rose said.

Before Rick could question that idea, Rose stepped over in front of Sobekneferu and took a knee.

"Mighty Pharaoh, daughter of Sobek. We beg forgiveness for trespassing in your sacred city. Since you have found it in your heart to forgive Mut-em-menu, we hope you can find it in your heart to forgive us."

Sobekneferu stopped the summoning chant for Sobek. Mut-em-menu realized she was chanting alone, and hers petered out. The crocodile bellowed as the transformation paused.

The spirit of Mut-em-menu grew brighter than Sobekneferu's. She glared at Rose. "Be silent, you jackal."

Then Sobekneferu brightened and her priestess dimmed. "Mut-em-menu has been my most loyal servant for years. Even now, after millennia, she has done as she has promised and returned us to Crocodopolis."

"And in the same way that earned her forgiveness for her disloyalty," Rose said, "we beg you to forgive our ignorance."

Sobekneferu's eyes narrowed. "What disloyalty?"

"My Queen," Mut-em-menu said, "there has been no disloyalty."

"You don't know?" Rose said. "The amulet from Mut-em-menu was taken from her mummified body, buried in the Valley of the Kings near your successor, Sobekhotep I."

The ethereal spirts of the two women drifted apart to either side of Donkor and faced each other.

"That's a lie," Mut-em-menu said. "During our escape, I stayed back to delay the army's advance with the powers given to me by the gods. I sacrificed my life and died to give you time to get to Crocodopolis."

Rose stood up. "But still, Mighty Queen, you didn't make it. The army's chariots caught up with you and caught you hiding in the escarpment, a location only Mut-em-menu knew."

"Yes," Sobekneferu said. "How could they know where I was?"

Mut-em-menu looked flustered. "They must have followed your trail through the desert."

"The trail my servants brushed away behind me?"

"She served the pharaoh who preceded you," Rose said. "She reveres Nekhbet, the duplicitous Vulture Queen. Why wouldn't she follow Nekhbet's example?"

"Yes, Mut-em-menu," Sobekneferu said. "You brought Nekhbet into our temples."

"At some point," Rose said, "she saw which way the wind was blowing, and decided to serve the next pharaoh after you as well. Survival drives her, not loyalty."

The pharaoh stared daggers at Mut-em-menu.

"And she brought us to you so she could survive again," Rose said. "She just needed you to help her do it."

"All those times you were out of the palace before the rebellion," Sobekneferu said, "they all make sense now."

"No, my Queen," Mut-em-menu said. "It wasn't like that."

"You viper. You plotted to have me killed from the beginning." The pharaoh reached through Donkor and wrapped her hands around Mut-em-menu's neck. "My father warned me not to trust you. I foolishly thought I was wiser than he."

Mut-em-menu choked. Her spirit dimmed and then brightened again.

"Queen of the Nile," she rasped out, "it was not my fault. I was captured, tortured. I was forced to tell them where you were."

"I know the general who was pursuing me. If that was true, he would have killed you after you betrayed me, infuriated by your weakness."

"It was all planned," Mut-em-menu sputtered. "I knew we would still be reunited, still bring Sobek back to rule."

"No one so treacherous deserves another moment outside of Duat," Sobekneferu said. "Your soul will weigh heavy in Ma'at's scale."

The pharaoh squeezed tighter. Mut-em-menu flashed and sizzled like an electrical short circuit.

"Now, Rick!" Rose said.

The two split and ran to the spears at the side of the room. He gripped the spear and felt an immediate surge of strength rush up his arms, into his chest and then down to his legs. Then he noticed there were two footprints beside him next to the pool. The stone was solid marble. There was no way feet could have made an impression in it. The edges of the impressions looked scorched. They uncomfortably reminded him of what a wall socket looked like after an electrical overload.

The last person to use this spear on Sobek channeled the power of the gods through his body, Rick thought. *I wonder if he survived?*

Across the pool, Rose had the other spear in her hands. If she also had footprints on her side, she'd be stepping in them right now. She lifted the spear as if it had only rested against the wall. She reared back to drive its point into the crocodile transforming into Sobek.

Rick wasn't about to let her do that alone. He stepped into the footprints and lifted the spear from its resting place. His eyes met Rose's. They nodded in unison. Then, in sync with his wife, they drove their spears into Sobek's sides.

CHAPTER TWENTY-SIX

Out in the Saharan wastes, Humphrey struggled to keep his rejuvenated motorcycle upright as it churned through the sand. The tracks left by Donkor and his men were straight and true compared to the one he was leaving behind. They were certainly better at driving across the dunes than he was. He consoled himself with the knowledge that they couldn't fly a plane.

Neither could they have fixed this motorcycle. Sand had worked its way into the gears of the kick-starter and locked it up. He'd had to disassemble it, repack it with grease, and put it back together. That had taken a long time.

He was afraid it had taken too long.

Sweat pasted his pack to his back. He wore his old flying goggles, but sand still managed to get under the seal and irritate his skin. As the sun roasted his hands, he wished he'd worn his flying gloves as well. He ran his tongue across his dry and cracking lips and swore he'd never let Rick talk him into another of his cockamamie schemes.

Ahead, the gang's motorcycle tracks ran up a large dune. Humphrey gunned his engine and followed them up, leaving a rooster tail of yellow sand flying behind him. He crested the top too quickly, and had to slide to a stop.

Two-thirds of the way up the dune across from him, Donkor's motorcycles lay beside a stretch of exposed, angled, white limestone. An opening in the middle looked like it led to whatever was inside the buried structure.

A set of footprints up the dune to that spot told Humphrey that the "whatever" included Rick and Rose.

He drove his motorcycle down his dune and up the next one. He continued past the opening. He parked it on the other side of the crest to hide it from Donkor and his men if they came out. Then he managed a clumsy, half-sliding descent to the limestone face. He listened and heard nothing within. He took a deep breath and stepped through the opening and onto a platform.

His eyes adjusted to the darkness just in time for him to not tumble down the stairway at the platform's side. He pulled a flashlight from his pack and clicked it on. The stairway descended several stories.

Good thing pilots don't have a fear of heights, he thought.

He descended the steps as fast as he could safely manage. At the bottom he was startled to discover the enormous statue of Sobek before what had been the original temple entrance. Behind the statue was the only way into the temple. A closer look revealed that that area was littered with an army of burned and crushed scorpions.

That did not bode well for what lay ahead. The good news was that Rick and Rose had survived the attack.

Beyond the scorpion graveyard was another set of steps. Light flickered at the bottom of those steps.

Humphrey turned off his flashlight and crept over to the stairs. Every crunch and squish of scorpion bodies sounded loud enough to alert Donkor and his goons to his arrival. At the top of the stairs, he peered down.

A lamp on the floor lit up the room. This stairway stopped at a corridor that stretched out for some distance. Water ran down a sluiceway in the center of the floor. Beside that sluiceway, a yard from the base of the steps, knelt one of Donkor's thugs. A bandoleer of ammo hung over one shoulder and across his back. He dipped his desert headdress in the running water and then ran it over his head and face. Then he stood and faced down that corridor, as if expecting his boss' return.

What he wasn't expecting was someone coming up from behind him.

He'd left his rifle leaning up against the far wall. Humphrey saw his chance.

He remembered his training from back in the Great War. He'd been taught how to sneak up behind a man, get him into a sleeper hold, and choke him out before he could warn anyone else. He hadn't had to execute the move since that training, and honestly never thought he would. Of course, he never thought he'd be in a buried Egyptian temple, so life was always full of surprises.

He descended the steps one at a time. The man was muttering to himself. Humphrey didn't understand the language, but he understood the tone. The man was scared and worried.

Humphrey paused at the base of the steps. He considered going for the rifle. It was too far away and looked like it had been around since Napoleon had ruled this place. He was going to have to count on the element of surprise.

He crept up behind the man. Humphrey's heart thudded in his chest and sweat broke out on his palms. He could smell the spicy meal the man had last eaten.

Humphrey took the last step quickly. He wrapped his right arm around the man's neck fast as lightning. He swung his left arm in to lock the hold.

His shirt hung up on the man's bandoleer. His sleeper hold turned into nothing more than a weak headlock.

Humphrey flashed back to his training on this particular move. His opponent had been shorter than he, not taller, like this guy was. He also hadn't been a practiced killer.

The henchman roared in anger. He grabbed Humphrey's arm with both hands and leaned forward. Humphrey came up off his feet. Given his weight, Humphrey couldn't help but be impressed. That feeling morphed immediately into terror.

The goon charged backward. Humphrey's half-assed headlock devolved into a panicked piggyback ride. They missed the steps and Humphrey's back slammed into a big circular handle on the wall. He felt things crunch in his spine. He screamed and lost his grip.

Humphrey dropped to the ground. The goon whirled around, eyes filled with fury. He sent a sandaled foot flying for Humphrey's face.

Humphrey ducked. The goon's foot struck the wall. Now the goon's foot made crunching sounds. The man wailed and hopped back on one foot.

Humphrey leapt to his feet, lowered a shoulder, and rushed the man like in his high school days as a defensive tackle.

But the gridiron hadn't had a sluiceway full of water running down it. Humphrey's foot slipped and splashed into it. He stumbled and leaned right. All he gave the hopping henchman was a glancing blow.

The man spun around on Humphrey and now it was Humphrey's turn to be in a headlock. It was a much better one than Humphrey had managed. The man squeezed and Humphrey choked. He wasn't going to last long like this.

He raised a foot and drove his heel down hard onto the man's injured foot. More bones crunched. The man wailed and relaxed his grip. Humphrey rotated and drove an elbow into the man's face. The thug moaned and staggered back.

The rifle leaned against the wall in front of him. Humphrey pounced on it. He turned in time to see the henchman rushing him with a dagger upraised in one hand. Humphrey raised the rifle by the barrel and prepared to clobber the thug.

The buttstock fell off and hit the ground with a thud. The trigger and receiver broke free. All Humphrey held was the skinny barrel.

Stabbed to death in a desert tomb was not how Humphrey wanted to leave this life.

CHAPTER TWENTY-SEVEN

In Sobek's temple room, Rick's spear pierced Sobek's side. Energy blasted through him like water through a firehose. His feet felt glued to the floor, his hands welded to the spear. A glow encompassed his body.

The two battling spirits of Sobekneferu and Mut-em-menu finally noticed Rick and Rose's skewering of Sobek. Sobekneferu released her priestess and broke into the resurrection chant again. Mut-em-menu recovered and then joined in.

Sobek bellowed and struggled against the spears plunged into his sides. As the women chanted, his transformation from crocodile to god restarted. Reptilian leather morphed into human-like skin and in moments he became all Sobek, with a great crocodile head and the powerful, muscled body of a man at least twelve feet tall. He wore a golden skirt and an intricate neckpiece of blue and yellow. A pharaonic-style headdress covered the back of his head. He snarled and twisted but the spears in his sides held firm. For now.

Across from Rick, Rose had been replaced. His wife had not only channeled the power of Horus through the spear, she had also channeled his appearance. Horus now held the weapon. The glow around his body lit up his feathered head. His eyes blazed with grim determination. Perhaps the god wanted Sobek to know who was defeating him again.

The two women continued shouting their incantation. Sobek grew in both size and strength. Rick felt the spear shudder in his hands. His arm muscles quivered on the verge of failing. He could feel the darker, evil force of

Sobek pushing the power he was channeling back down the spear. On the other side, Rose-as-Horus struggled to keep on her feet as well.

They were going to lose this fight.

Then the floor shuddered, as if an earthquake had come. The platform in the pool shimmied and collapsed the remaining catwalk to it with a splash. Donkor swayed back and forth, and with him the two spirits.

Suddenly, from out of the pool burst Colin. Or at least a ghostly image of Colin. He flew to the platform and landed next to Donkor. Colin plunged his hand into Donkor's chest where the twin amulets glowed within. His hand closed around them and they dimmed.

Sobekneferu and Mut-em-menu shrieked and lunged for Colin.

"This is mine!" Colin yanked the amulet out of Donkor's body. Blood gushed from the ragged hole left behind.

The women grabbed Colin.

The three spirits twisted and flowed in strange shapes. Then they began to swirl and melded into a horrific vision of six grappling arms and three furious faces. The light from the pendant glowed fiercely in the center of the storm. The spirits spun into a tornado and wind sent bits of stinging sand swirling through the air.

The light in the amulet went out. The queen and her priestess screamed in pain and frustration. Then all three spirits vanished. Donkor keeled over off the back of the platform and landed in the pool.

In an instant, the power coursing through Rick surged. His muscles turned strong as steel.

Across from him, the glow around Rose-as-Horus intensified.

Sobek roared with anger. The skin around where the spears pierced him on both sides turned black, and then glowed red. Twin wildfires erupted from the wounds and spread in a flash, leaving behind charred, immobile skin. The circles of spreading flames met in the center of the god's chest.

Sobek's frustrated roar became a wail of pain. Flames spread up his chest, out his arms, and down his legs, even somehow burning underwater. A necklace of fire swept up to the base of his skull. Sobek raised his eyes skyward and howled as the flames consumed his head. The fire died away and left behind a blackened face, frozen in a scream of open-mouthed agony.

Then as if exploded from within, the entire body disintegrated into dust that vanished before it hit the pool.

Suddenly Rick's spear felt like it weighed a thousand pounds. He dropped it. The weapon hit and cracked the corner of the pool wall.

Across the way, Rose had dropped her spear as well and leaned against the pool's edge. She looked as exhausted as Rick felt.

In the pool, Donkor floated face up with a hole ripped in his chest. Blood stained the still water around him. Wreckage of the walkways lay in the water, but there was no sign of the crocodile, the amulets, or anything else.

Out in the corridor, the crocodile crawled back to its room, as if no longer compelled to guard duty by the Egyptian spirits.

"How are you doing, Rosie?" Rick said.

"For someone who just sent a god back to prison, pretty good. You?"

"I think I'll sleep for a week when we get home."

"I'll join you in that," Rose said.

"I was pleasantly surprised to have Colin's spirit arrive and give us a hand."

"Maybe the two spirits on the platform kept some kind of doorway to the spirit world open for Colin to pass through," Rose said. "Do you think Colin's spirit crossed over to help us or to get vengeance against Donkor?"

"I'm thinking the latter. But the result is more important than the motive as far as I'm concerned. He was the card we needed to fill our inside straight."

Rick gripped the spear. It felt cold and inert, which he interpreted as safe.

"These will be the perfect artifacts to bring home," he said. "They will display well and should get a great price, especially selling the pair together."

Rick tried to lift the spear. It once more felt like it weighed a thousand pounds.

"Can you move yours?" he said.

Rose gave hers a tug. "Not an inch. Maybe that's why they were still here when we opened this place up. Left here by Horus and Anubis to thwart anyone trying to free Sobek."

Rick met Rose at the head of the pool. They hugged and kissed and he hadn't ever felt anything better.

"Speaking of Horus, you looked just like him when we were skewering Sobek. Feathers are not your best look."

Rose stifled a laugh. "That's coming from a man with a dog's head."

"What?"

"You looked like Anubis, and it will take a long time for me to see you as anything else."

"Ha-ha. Let's get those scaled armor plates and get out of this place. I'm betting Humphrey is lounging around back at the plane bored stiff."

***

Back at the water gate, Donkor's henchman ran at Humphrey full speed with his knife raised high. Even if he didn't stab Humphrey to death, he was about to crush the life out of him against the wall. Smacking the man with the gun barrel wasn't going to stop him.

In desperation, Humphrey grabbed the gun barrel with his right hand and launched it at the henchman like he was throwing a dart.

Between the narrow profile and the poor light, the henchman didn't seem to see the steel tube flying toward him.

The barrel struck him dead in the center of his forehead. His eyes crossed, he moaned, and dropped the knife. Then he tumbled to the ground and lay there unconscious.

"Buddy," Humphrey said, "you're gonna thank me later for beaning you. If'n you'd tried to shoot me with that rickety rifle, it'd have done killed you."

A bellowing noise echoed from down the corridor. The hairs on Humphrey's arms went to attention. Humphrey had spent enough nights in the swamps outside Savannah to recognize the roar of an alligator, and he bet a crocodile sounded about the same.

Sure enough, a crocodile came dashing down the corridor straight for him. Its tail splashed in the sluiceway with each step.

Now Humphrey didn't even have the gun barrel for protection. He couldn't outrun the croc to the supposed safety of the staircase, but he was sure as hell going to try.

He bolted for the steps. The crocodile closed the gap.

Humphrey made it to the first step and heard an awful snap and crunch sound.

He looked down. He still had both feet and legs.

He spun around in time to see the crocodile dragging the henchman's body down the corridor. The beast disappeared through a doorway on the right.

Humphrey caught his breath and gave his heart a moment to slow down. He realized how unnatural it was to have living crocodiles inside a temple buried for centuries. It was also unnatural to have water running through it. He knew he wasn't the brightest bulb on the Christmas tree, but he bet those two things were related.

The fact that Donkor had left the late and unlamented henchman to guard the source told him it was important to keep that water flowing. Humphrey figured whatever was good for Donkor had to be bad for Rick and Rose.

He hopped off the steps and went to the water source. The water flowed over the top of a big brass plate like the spillway for a dam. Rose had talked about Crocodopolis being watered by the Nile, but this door tapped into an underground spring like an oasis did. A wheel on the right looked like it raised and lowered the door.

Humphrey stepped over to the wheel. It was awfully crooked. He remembered the henchman slamming him into something. He bet he had a nice circular bruise on his back just the size of that wheel.

He grabbed the wheel with both hands and twisted.

It didn't move.

Bending it must have jammed up the gears. He moved his feet shoulder-width apart, squatted, and this time threw his whole body into the effort.

The wheel turned. Then it sheared off its mounts and left him holding it.

"Well, that dog sure won't hunt no more."

The gears along the edge of the door moaned. The ones the wheel had controlled snapped one after another.

The gate slid down. A Niagara-grade waterfall rushed out over the top. It hit the ground near Humphrey's feet and the backsplash soaked him. He plastered himself against the wall as the torrent funneled down the corridor and headed for wherever Rick and Rose were.

CHAPTER TWENTY-EIGHT

Rick turned to head for the chariot room and the scaled armor breastplates.

Rose stopped him with a hand against his chest. "Are you sure we should take that armor?"

"We don't have a choice. We can't leave without it. Literally, we need it to pay for gas to get home."

"But this is such a huge discovery. The Egyptians will prize the armor of Sobekneferu. Archeologists will want to preserve all of it."

Rick patted Rose's arm. "And we'll leave them this whole complex, including the statue, the scorpion bodies, and the corpse in the pool. They can set up a picnic right here."

"And you're forgetting the curse of Tutankhamen."

"I didn't read any curses inscribed anywhere."

"Because you don't read hieroglyphics," Rose said. "These walls could be filled with warnings. And since we just saw three Egyptian gods fight it out in front of a pair of millennia old ghosts, you can't dismiss that this place is infested with the supernatural."

"Rosie, we just sent a god back to whatever the Egyptian version of Hell is and we sent two ghosts packing for the Afterlife. I think we're safe for a while."

A rumbling noise came from up the corridor.

"Rick, did you hear that?"

The water in the sluiceway swelled and overflowed onto the floor. Then a foot-high wave of water rushed in across the floor and sent them calf-deep in it.

"That brass gate must have failed," Rose said.

Rick turned to face the chariot room. "I'll grab the..."

Water had already surged into the room. Chunks of chariot bobbed out the doorway.

"The armor is already washed away." Rose pulled on his arm. "Soon we'll be."

Rick gave the chariot room one last, longing look, muttered a curse, and then turned for the corridor. He looked into the pool and found the rifle the henchman had dragged in with him. Rick pulled it out.

"Donkor might have more thugs waiting for us outside," he said.

"If you don't hurry, we'll never make it outside."

He and Rose waded upstream against the rushing water. It was already to their knees.

"Once this water gets higher than the sides of the pools…" Rose said.

A crocodile roared in one of the upstream rooms. Rick's pulse spiked. Then a snout peeked out from the doorway.

"You had to jinx us, didn't you?" Rick pushed Rose back into the room behind them. Then he aimed the rifle upstream.

The crocodile's head and forelegs came out of the door. The current grabbed it and pulled it into the stream like pulling a cork from a wine bottle.

Rick put the croc in his sights and fired.

The old rifle kicked hard against his shoulder. Its sharp report echoed off the walls.

The round caught the crocodile in the side of the head and sent a spray of blood and brains over the water. Like a capsizing battleship, the crocodile rolled over until it was belly up in the water. Rick backed into the doorway he'd pushed Rose into. The current floated the corpse past them.

"Scratch one croc," Rick said.

He grabbed the bolt to cycle in a new round. It didn't move. The casing had jammed, water had locked the mechanism, or maybe the old rifle mechanism had just shattered.

"Bad news," Rick said.

Behind them in their room, a crocodile hissed. Rick swiveled his head in that direction. A large crocodile had his head and forelegs out of the pool in the room.

"Worse news," Rose said.

Once the crocodile was fully out of the pool, this game was over. Rick had one last chance and he needed to take it now.

He charged the croc.

"Rick, no!" Rose yelled.

Its jaws opened wide. He rammed the rifle down the creature's throat until the buttstock was between its teeth. He pulled his hands away just as the crocodile clamped its jaws shut. The wooden stock splintered.

The crocodile hissed in fury and whipped back and forth, trying to dislodge the rifle. Blood pumped from its mouth.

Rose grabbed Rick by the belt and tugged. "Let's go!"

The two left the flailing, weakening crocodile in the room and moved into the corridor. Rick pushed Rose ahead of him. The water was waist-high and still moving fast. That meant Rick and Rose were moving slower, and the water kept rising. If another crocodile came swimming by now, they'd had it.

They neared the corridor's end. The steps were in sight. But Rick was exhausted. His pounding heart and burning legs had had enough. The rushing water kept making his feet slip against the floor. He and Rose flattened their backs against the wall to help avoid the current.

Rose lost her footing. The current swept her past Rick.

He shot one arm out and grabbed her under the armpit. It took all his strength to pull her in to his side. She struggled to keep upright beside him. The rising water almost covered her chest.

"We're not going to make it," she said.

Rick pulled her close. "If you think this is how our story ends, you're crazy. We're going to get out of here."

"That's going to take a miracle."

Rick had to admit to himself he wasn't going to have time to fake it before he figured out a way out of this mess.

Three of the lamp oil amphorae floated by, and then stopped just past them. The handles were bound together by a rope that went back upstream.

"Behold," Rick said. "One miracle."

"Ricky?" Humphrey's voice rang out. "You down there somewheres?"

"Humphrey!" Rick bent over to see the steps. Humphrey sat on the steps that were still above the water with the end of a rope in his hands. A lantern burned beside him.

"Rose and I are here," Rick called out. "The water's running too fast for us."

"Grab them jugs and the rope. You walk, I'll pull, and we'll get out of this place."

Rick gave Rose a squeeze. "Ready, Rosie?"

Rose took a deep breath. "Ready."

Rick wrapped an arm around her waist and the two of them waded out into the water. The current almost sent him skidding back. Water lapped at his neck. Two agonizing steps in, and he wasn't sure they were going to make it. He twisted to get Rose closer to the rope.

"Grab it, Rosie."

Rose reached out. The amphorae bobbed out of reach. Rick managed a half step more. The amphorae floated closer. Rose grabbed the rope.

She spit out a mouthful of water. "Got it!"

Rose pulled the rope in close. Rick let her go and grabbed it with both hands. Up on the steps, Humphrey began to pull it in hand over hand while Rick and Rose walked forward. The water continued to rise.

Rick and Rose finally made it to the stairway as the water reached their chins. They climbed up the steps on all fours, exhausted. Humphrey helped them up and they collapsed in the corridor behind the Sobek statue. Rick landed on dead scorpions. He didn't care.

"Humphrey," Rose said, "you saved us. There was a door holding back the spring water. It must have broken."

Humphrey scratched his head under his hat. "Yep. Must have broken."

"How did you find us?" Rick said.

"Donkor and his men found the plane, but they didn't find me. They had this trained vulture that was like a scout for them. They followed it to you, and I followed them."

"They're still down there," Rick said, pointing down the fully-flooded corridor. "They won't be coming back."

"And Colin?"

"He won't be, either."

"Ricky, tell me you got us some treasure, though."

Rick winced. "Sorry. No luck there."

"I think our lives are more valuable than treasure," Rose said.

"Not to the man selling aviation fuel," Humphrey said.

The whole temple trembled.

"Now what?" Rick said.

"The water," Rose said. "It's filling the temple and it weighs a lot more than air. Add in the sand weighing down on top of it and this foundation can't handle the weight. The temple's breaking up."

CHAPTER TWENTY-NINE

Rose had survived a battle between gods, the wrath of ghosts, and a sea of scorpions. She hadn't made it through all that to be buried alive in an Egyptian temple.

The three jumped to their feet and headed for the staircase to the exit. Rose almost cheered as she spied light still streaming through the opening. That meant the temple hadn't buried itself.

Yet.

Just as the three made it to the bottom step, the temple floor sagged left with an awful grinding noise. Pieces of the roof broke free, hurtled down to the floor, and hit with a crash.

One section dropped onto the upper stairway. It sheared away a three-yard-long section of steps. A cascade of broken stone rained down. Rose covered her head and turned away. The stone blocks hit the floor and shattered. Pebbles peppered Rose's body. When the pelting stopped, she looked up to see an insurmountable gap now separated the two sections of the stairway.

"Now what?" Rose said.

The temple rumbled again. Sand poured through the gaps in the roof and that reminded her uncomfortably like an hourglass.

Rick sized up the Sobek statue. The last shift in the foundation gave it a slight forward tilt.

"Sit tight," he said. "I have a plan."

Those three words never inspired her confidence.

Rick dashed off, and then returned with the rope that Humphrey had saved them with.

"How's that gonna help?" Humphrey said.

"I'm going to call in help from Sobek." Rick began to tie the end of the rope into a loop.

"We just sent that god back to some underworld prison," Rose said.

"Not that god." Rick pointed up to the statue. "That one. We're going to topple it forward. It should hit the wall right above the break in the stairs. We climb the statue and get out of here."

"How are you going to…"

Rick finished tying the end of the rope into a Honda knot and a second later he had a lasso.

"Oh, no," Rose said. "You're kidding."

"Aw, Rick," Humphrey said. "I seen you trying to rope things. We need another plan."

"Humphrey, Rosie, prepare to be impressed."

"By impressed you mean crushed to death in a collapsing temple?" Rose said.

The temple shifted again. Stones along the far wall cracked and sent shards of rock flying down.

"Step back and let a man work, Rosie."

Rick whipped the lasso into a twirl over his head. Then he sent the loop sailing up to the head of the Sobek statue. It hit the statue's neck and dropped back to the floor.

"Rick!" Rose said.

"Just getting the range, honey." He re-coiled the rope. "Here we go."

He sent the lasso up again. This time it landed on the statue's head. Rick drew it tight and it bound the head right above the snout.

"That was a thousand-to-one shot," Rose said.

"Those are my specialty," Rick said. "Now everyone pull."

The three of them grabbed the rope and pulled. The only thing that moved were their feet across the sandy floor.

The temple shifted again. Huge splashes echoed from the lower level as blocks toppled into the rising water. The lantern they'd left in the passage went out.

"All together this time," Rick said. "One…two…three!"

The three pulled. Rose's muscles strained, but the statue didn't budge.

The floor beneath them cracked and sagged. The forward ankle of the statue shattered. The Sobek statute began to topple in their direction.

The three released the rope and scrambled out of the way. The statue did what looked like a slow-motion fall. The rear ankle snapped and the statue landed on the stumps of its legs. The head struck the wall face-first and the snout exploded into dust and bits. The head buried itself in the wall, and right under the stairway.

Rick rested a hand on Rose's shoulder. "See, what did I tell you?"

"That plan worked by sheer, dumb luck."

"What do I always say, Humphrey?"

Humphrey sighed. "Better to be lucky than good."

"Bingo. Let's climb."

Rick let Rose go first. Sobek's body was slick, but there were enough details chiseled into his clothing that she could find some hand and foot holds. As she climbed, more sounds of collapse came up from the passageway. She finally made it to the steps and turned to help Rick who was a half-dozen feet behind her.

"Don't wait on us, Rosie. Get out. I'm right behind you."

Rose climbed the remaining stairs to the entrance. When she turned around, Rick was already on the staircase and Humphrey was climbing across Sobek's head.

The temple shook again. She stepped out into the blazing sunlight. Rose squinted and shaded her eyes.

Water bubbled in the depression between the dunes. Deep groaning noises came from the surrounding dunes as the sand in them shifted. Rick and Humphrey stepped up behind her. Both were panting.

"The temple was the centerpiece of Crocodopolis," Rose said. "Its collapse is weakening the foundations of all the other buildings. And that spring is more like an underground Nile tributary. All that water is turning the ground into something closer to quicksand. We need to get as far away as we can."

"I got us some rides," Humphrey said. He pointed to two motorcycles near the entrance. "Mine's on the other side of this dune. You know how to ride, Miss Rose?"

Rose shook her head. "On one of those deathtraps? I'd be safer back in the temple."

"She can ride with me," Rick said. "Show us the way back to the plane."

Humphrey ran up the hill and vanished. Then came the roar of a motorcycle. Humphrey crested the hill on a bike and rode down to where the other two were waiting.

Rick surveyed the remaining two. He picked the one with the widest seat, mounted it, and fired it up.

He waved Rose over.

"I'm only doing this to save my life," she said. "I'm still not riding with you on yours when we get home."

"Deal."

She got on behind Rick and wrapped her arms around his waist.

"Good thing you aren't wearing a skirt," he said.

The ground shook and dropped several feet. The two men gunned the motorcycles and they peeled out in a spray of sand. Rose hung on for dear life.

The motorcycles crested the dune and sped up on the downslope. Rose looked over her shoulder to see the dunes behind her collapsing into what looked like a cauldron of boiling water. Rick and Humphrey stopped on solid ground.

The last of the dunes submerged into the roiling lake. Then the water went still and began to percolate back into the ground. In moments, a mirage-like shimmer distorted the place. When it dissipated, all that remained was flat desert. Crocodopolis was gone without leaving a trace.

"And just like that," Rose said, "it's all gone. No one will believe we ever found Crocodopolis."

"As if we would ever tell anyone," Rick said.

"Yeah," Humphrey said, "folks might be mad about us sinking their lost city."

"It takes a lot to sink a city," Rose said. "You think Anubis and Horus might have had a hand in what just happened?"

"They had a hand in skewering Sobek," Rick said. "I wouldn't put it past them."

"What are you guys talking about?" Humphrey said.

"You know how I always say that my wife is a goddess?" Rick said. "Well for a moment back in the temple, she really was."

CHAPTER THIRTY.

Humphrey's assessment of their fuel situation had been dead-on. They'd taken off from the site of Crocodopolis and made it back to the airstrip with little more than fumes in the tank. Rick's wallet was also on fumes, so that meant an uncomfortable night sleeping in the plane for everyone. Rick dozed off that night hoping that after a good night's sleep he would awaken with an amazing plan to get them home.

The morning came, but an amazing plan did not.

The sun burned red and low on the horizon. He and Humphrey sat on chairs under the wing drinking coffee Humphrey had brewed on a tiny stove. Rose still slept in the plane and Rick wasn't about to wake her. She certainly deserved the rest.

"I'm going to nominate this coffee as worst in the world," Rick said.

"This ain't no Pan Am Clipper," Humphrey said. "You're on a working man's plane."

"We're going to need some kind of work if we're ever going to buy enough gas to get home."

"You know what people get paid in this country? It would take all three of us working for a year to fill up the tank."

Rick scratched his chin. "The high-end hotels have got off-the-books gambling going on each night. I think I could play my way to a few tanks of fuel."

"Sure. If someone granted you a grubstake, and you had the clothes to pass yourself off as rich, and you knew whatever the secret password was to get through the door. Heck, Ricky, I'll start counting the money right now."

"That kind of negative thinking just invites bad luck," Rick said. "I've got a gut feeling we're about to turn this whole thing around."

A Rolls Royce pulled up to the end of what passed as a parking apron at this airport. The red car sported black above the doors and on the fenders, which made the bright red seem even brighter. The sun glinted off the polished radiator and the enormous hood ornament. A driver got out and then opened the rear door.

Out stepped a middle-aged man in a white linen coat and slacks. He wore a straw boater hat and carried a cane. He glanced at the Tri-motor, exchanged a few words with his driver, then approached the plane.

Rick sat up straight in his seat. He'd been dreading the arrival of some British official who was going to make their situation even worse.

The man had a narrow face, olive skin, and hair black as a raven's feathers. Even at a distance, his black eyes seemed to look right through Rick.

"You've seen this guy before?" Rick said.

"Nope. And from the looks of him, I ain't in no hurry to see him now."

The man stopped a few feet from them and tipped his hat. "Gentlemen. Is one of you the pilot?"

Rick was surprised that the man had a Greek accent.

"That's me," Humphrey said.

The time to bluff had come. Rick stood up. "But I'm the one who's chartered the plane."

"*Eimai tyheros*," the man said with a smile. "I am Sideris Lazaridis."

"I'm Rick Sinclair. This is Humphrey Custis."

"A pleasure to meet you both. Your tail numbers are American. You are returning to America soon?"

And negotiations have just opened, Rick thought.

"Actually," he said, "we were planning on taking off when we finished our coffee."

"I am here on holiday from Greece and am not returning until next week. But there is something I'd like to send home as soon as possible. Perhaps you could route your flight through one of our islands and take it for me?"

"Why don't you take it?"

"It is bulky, and I am returning home on a liner. Such luggage isn't really encouraged on a passenger ship so I'd like to avoid that bother."

"And the Customs people on both ends of the trip?"

The man smiled. "Americans are known for their directness. Yes, a Customs inspection would be time consuming."

"And that's the rub," Rick said. "Greece is out of our way. Plus, our trip here is on the up-and-up. We would need a significant inducement to do anything the authorities may frown upon."

"Mr. Sinclair, to be candid, an old airplane with faded tail numbers parked at an unregulated airstrip does not seem very 'up-and-up', as you put it. However, I am willing to pay top dollar for this service."

Lazaridis quoted a price that would have bought enough gas not only to get them home, but to get them around the world if they wanted to. Rick tried to mask his excitement.

"We'll need to be paid in advance," Rick said.

"You are not the postal service. I will give you 25% now, and the remainder on delivery."

Rick wondered if that would buy enough gas to get them to Greece. He looked over to Humphrey, who was giving him a furious head-bobbing "yes" about taking the deal.

"You have a deal," Rick said.

The two shook hands. Rick was filled with dread at the man's touch. He chalked it up to being tired.

Lazaridis pulled a wad of bills from his pocket and peeled off a handful of large denomination American dollars. He handed them to Rick. Then he waved to his driver who was still standing beside the Rolls.

The driver nodded, went to the trunk, and pulled out a crate three feet long, a foot wide, and two feet tall. Rope handles hung on each side. He hoisted up the crate and brought it over to the group. He set it down by the tailwheel and went back to the car.

"What's in the crate?" Humphrey said.

"Something that is only of value to myself and my family. Your high rate of pay includes keeping the box sealed."

"We can do that," Rick said.

"There is an airfield on the island of Serafina, west of Kriti, or Crete as you call it. Land there. The security is infamously lax. If you tell them you are just refueling and leaving in the morning, they will take your word for it."

"They sound very trusting."

"No, very corrupt. They just assume everyone is smuggling something and have been paid to look the other way. After sunset, deliver the crate to the address written on the box. My daughter will pay you the rest of your fee."

"Well, *you're* very trusting, then. What's to keep us from taking your money and flying home?"

Lazaridis broke into a grin that chilled Rick's blood. "If I can find you in Cairo, Mr. Sinclair, I can certainly find you in Savannah. *A'dio*."

Lazaridis turned on his heel and went back to the Rolls. The driver was waiting with the rear door open.

"Uh, Rick," Humphrey said, "how did he know we lived in Savannah?"

"He must have seen it on some paperwork you filed."

"Does this look like the kind of airport that has paperwork? Look, I've dealt with some shady fellas over the years. That man might dress nice, but I'll bet he's crooked as a hound dog's leg and twice as dirty."

"Of course he is. Why else would he want us to ship that crate?"

"I'm used to knowing at least half the folks I'm dealing with on one of these here off-the-books shipments. This time I don't know nobody."

"Look, we're in a jam here. We were going to stop in Greece anyway."

"Sicily, actually."

"Whatever. The point is we have money for fuel to get there and once we drop off the box, we'll turn a profit on this entire fiasco. How can we turn that down?"

"You know, my momma's side of the family is Greek."

"Excellent! So, you speak Greek?"

"No, but thanks to Grandma's cooking, I can eat Greek."

"Well," Rick said, "that's a start."

"You know Miss Rose ain't gonna like this plan."

"We don't even have to tell her. We tuck the crate in your secret compartment now. After we land in Serafina, we'll sneak it out to the address at night while she's sleeping."

"Let me count the number of things you've been able to keep secret from Miss Rose." Humphrey pantomimed counting on his fingers. "Zero, that's how many."

"There's a first time for everything."

Humphrey rubbed the back of his neck. "Well, I sure hope this is it, because she's gonna be madder than a wet hen if she finds out."

Rick knew Humphrey was right about that. But he had a good feeling about this plan. It couldn't be simpler.

How much trouble could they get into delivering a little box?

AFTERWORD

Those were a few more close calls for Rick, Rose, and Humphrey, but it looks like they survived another adventure.

The inspiration for this story came to me when I was visiting Gatorland in Orlando, Florida. The place is literally teeming with alligators and crocodiles of all species. There are gator feeding shows and lots of other animal show entertainment. Any fan of large reptiles should visit there when they are in Central Florida.

There is a Nile crocodile exhibit near the back of the park and next to it were several signs talking about the crocs' attributes and their role in Ancient Egypt. The signs mentioned a city built to worship a crocodile-headed god named Sobek. I was halfway through writing Rick and Rose's second adventure *Voyage to Blackbeard's Island* and the idea of discovering the lost city of Crocodopolis seemed like something Rick would get them into. So, I took pictures of the crocodiles and the signs to remind me of the idea.

But *Voyage to Blackbeard's Island* ended up to have crocodiles in it and I didn't want the series to turn into the Crocodile Chronicles. So, the idea went to the back burner and was replaced with what became the vampire tale *Search for the City of Gold*. A Southeast Asian inspiration hit me as I was finishing that one, and *Passage Up the Mekong* was born. After finishing that novel, I came across the pictures I'd taken and remembered Crocodopolis. So, two novels after the idea came to me, here it is.

There is a lot of real history leavened into this fiction, so let's dive into it.

We'll start with Sobek, the real-life crocodile-headed god of Ancient Egypt. There are countless stories of him letting emotions trump reason in the River Nile, and so he's one of the most dangerous Egyptian gods.

According to the mythos, Osiris' brother Seth murdered Osiris, chopped up the corpse into 14 parts, and dumped it in the Nile.

Apparently not one to let a good meal go to waste, Sobek devoured Osiris' body parts. Sobek was brought before the council of Egyptian gods and tried for this sacrilegious act. He was found guilty and punished by having his tongue cut off.

Sobekneferu, also known as Neferusobek, was a real Egyptian pharaoh and the first woman to rule. Most of the story related about her in the novel is correct. She did only rule for a few years and the details around why her rule ended are murky. But a coup against a woman ruler who turned the Egyptian hierarchy of deities upside down is certainly plausible. Pharaohs had been overthrown for far less. From what I can find, her burial place remains lost to history.

Now why she chose to turn Egypt to worshiping the evil Sobek is a mystery. Maybe she thought the first female pharaoh needed to start new traditions. Maybe she just identified more with the bad guys. For whatever reason, she devoted resources from her waning empire into building Crocodopolis for him.

Greek historian Herodotus confirmed that Crocodopolis did exist and that he had been there. He wrote:

"...no words can tell its wonders ... were all that Greeks have builded (sic) *and wrought added together the whole would be seen to be a matter of less labor and cost than was this labyrinth..."*

He claimed that the city was a labyrinth of around 1,500 double sets of chambers plus underground chambers containing "the burial vaults of the kings who first built this labyrinth, and [those] of the sacred crocodiles."

Herodotus says he visited the place during a trip to the now evaporated Lake Moeris. Such a vast structure still hasn't been discovered, though excavations carried out there in 1910 by British archaeologist Sir Finders Petrie recovered several statues and reliefs of Sobek.

Colin's grandmother in the story is Florence Farr. She was a real British stage actress who lived between 1860 and 1917. She was a member of the Hermetic Order of the Golden Dawn and did indeed claim to channel a "chantress" named Mut-em-menu. She considered Mut-em-menu her "ka" or sister-self. An offshoot group known as "The Sphere" focused on channeling Mut-em-menu and reviving the powerful magics of Ancient Egypt. One historian believes that Bram Stoker knew her, or at least knew of her, and that she was one of the main influences behind the character of Margaret Trelawny in Stoker's *The Jewel of the Seven Stars*. While she did die in 1917, there was no mystery about her death and there was no unrealized trip to Egypt.

There is mention in the story of the supposed Curse of Tutankhamen that killed multiple members of the expedition that opened his tomb. In the years after the opening, that rumor was often accepted as fact and widely published in credible sources. But in 1934 Egyptologist Herbert Winlock compiled a chart, published in The New York Times. Twelve years after the opening of the tomb only six of the 40 people present at the opening had died. More recently, an epidemiologist compared the lifespans of people who were in the tomb with people who were in Egypt but not in the tomb. His 2002 report, published in the British Medical Journal, concluded that the studied individuals lived on average for more than 20 years after the tomb was opened, whether they entered it or not.

Sorry Universal monster movies fans, no mummy's curse.

The descriptions of 1938 Cairo are as accurate as I could make them without a time machine. But I did find something close. An old travel newsreel made in Cairo at that time is available on YouTube. Give a search and you'll find it. It's really cool if you are into history.

That's about it for the backstories. Thanks to the amazing folks at Severed Press for editing and the killer cover art that turns these tales from unseen manuscripts to books on your shelves.

Now what do you think is in that crate Rick is taking to Greece? You can bet whatever it is will start them on a new adventure and it won't make Rose happy in the least. Sign up for my monthly newsletter at my website www.russellrjames.com and you will be the first to know when the next Rick and Rose Sinclair adventure is ready to read. While you wait, check out the Grant Coleman series and the Ranger Kathy West series at my website. Those two sets of adventure tales might tide you over.

I travel the United States doing book signings at cons. That schedule is also on my website. Hope to meet you at one of those, but you can always email me at rrj@russellrjames.com to say hi as well.

Thanks for reading my work and I'll talk to you again soon.

-Russell James

Made in the USA
Coppell, TX
13 June 2026

81356207R00098